A child. Tom had

Numbly, Marnie stared down at the moppet. Although the little boy's hair was lighter than Tom's, there was no denying the resemblance.

Marnie supposed it was possible he'd fallen for a woman on the rebound, but she refused to fool herself. She'd known all along Tom would want children when he found the right mate.

No wonder no one had told her. It hurt like fire to know that the man she loved had so easily found happiness with someone else. Still, it was cruel of him to spring it on her this way. Her voice trembling, Marnie said, "I don't see what's so difficult about sending a wedding announcement."

"I'm not married," he murmured as his son padded down the hall ahead of them.

CR   Br

Dear Reader,

As the hectic holiday season begins, take a moment to treat yourself to a fantastic love story from Harlequin American Romance. All four of our wonderful books this month are sure to please your every reading fancy.

Beloved author Cathy Gillen Thacker presents us with *A Cowboy Kind of Daddy*, the fourth and final title in her series THE McCABES OF TEXAS. Travis McCabe is the last eligible bachelor in the family and you know his matchmaking parents are not about to let him miss heading to the altar.

Also wrapping up this month is our special series DELIVERY ROOM DADS. Judy Christenberry's memorable *Baby 2000* has a truly heroic McIntyre brother caring for an expectant mother who just may have the first baby of the millennium.

Two holiday stories finish up the month with tales that will bring you lots of seasonal joy. Pamela Bauer pens a delightful small-town romance with *Saving Christmas*, and Jacqueline Diamond brings us an emotional story of unexpected reunions with *Mistletoe Daddy*.

Here's hoping your holiday season is filled with happiness, good health—and lots of romance!

Melissa Jeglinski
Associate Senior Editor

Mistletoe
Daddy

JACQUELINE DIAMOND

HARLEQUIN®

TORONTO • NEW YORK • LONDON
AMSTERDAM • PARIS • SYDNEY • HAMBURG
STOCKHOLM • ATHENS • TOKYO • MILAN • MADRID
PRAGUE • WARSAW • BUDAPEST • AUCKLAND

ISBN 0-373-16804-7

MISTLETOE DADDY

Copyright © 1999 by Jackie Hyman.

This edition published by arrangement with Harlequin Books S.A.

® and TM are trademarks of the publisher. Trademarks indicated with ® are registered in the United States Patent and Trademark Office, the Canadian Trade Marks Office and in other countries.

Visit us at www.romance.net

Printed in U.S.A.

ABOUT THE AUTHOR

Although Jacqueline Diamond now lives in Southern California, she grew up in Tennessee, where this story is set. She also lived briefly in Italy, and has great affection for the Italian language, culture and music. You can write to Jackie at P.O. Box 1315, Brea, CA 92822.

Books by Jacqueline Diamond

HARLEQUIN AMERICAN ROMANCE

In loving memory of Cheryl Hyman

Chapter One

Marnie Afton was gift wrapping a romance novel for a customer when the phone rang. As she answered, she glanced at the hand-carved wall clock and noticed it was still an hour before closing time.

"Afton Books, Stationery and Gifts, can I help you?" Tucking the handset between her shoulder and cheek, she topped the package with a silver bow and two tiny teddy bears.

Her grandmother didn't bother to say hello. "He's here."

Marnie's arm jerked so hard she knocked over a small rack of bookmarks next to the cash register. She hurried to straighten it. "Already?"

"He rented a car in Nashville and drove straight from the airport," said Jolene Afton.

"But he was supposed to wait and share a ride with Uncle Norbert and Aunt Linda!" Marnie's gaze swept the bright, spacious store. The only customer was the woman waiting in front of her. No Christmas shoppers lingered among the displays of books and computer games, thank goodness. She could afford to close a little early.

"He must have been impatient to get here," her grandmother went on. "You aren't going to leave that man standing around thinking you're still mad at him, are you?"

"No. No...I just—" Marnie swallowed hard. Until this moment, she'd believed she was finally ready to face her ex-husband, for the first time in four years. An image of Tom flashed into her mind: intense blue eyes, tanned skin, an unruly mop of dark-blond hair. She could smell the musky aftershave he'd worn since high school, the one that used to make her weak in the knees.

But she was no longer the naive young girl whose pulse sped up at the subtle defiance in Tom Jakes's hard body and at the veiled invitation in his glance. She was thirty-two years old and in charge of her life.

"I think you've decorated that well enough," her customer said mildly. The woman, a teacher at the new elementary school just outside town, gave Marnie an indulgent smile.

"Oh!" Looking down, she saw that she'd started to apply a second bow. "Well, happy holidays! I know your sister will enjoy the book. It's one of my favorites."

"Mine, too. Have a good time at your grandmother's." Collecting the gift and her receipt, the woman went out through the frosted-glass door.

"Marnie?" demanded the voice on the phone. "You know that being kept waiting isn't good for my heart."

"Now, please, don't excite yourself. I'm about to lock up." Marnie shifted position and bumped the display shelves behind her. From high up, something large and furry plummeted onto her head.

She grabbed the teddy bear before it hit the floor and nearly dropped the phone in the process. "Granny? I'm sorry!"

"I don't think my old system can take all this suspense," Jolene warned in her ear.

"I have to close out the cash register and turn off the computer." Marnie hoisted the bear back onto its shelf. "Betty's working tomorrow and on Christmas Eve, but I need to leave everything in good shape."

It went against her nature to take off two whole days before the holiday, but Jolene had insisted on it. Besides, although Marnie had been hearing complaints about her grandmother's heart for years, Jolene's increasingly frequent references to it were worrisome.

"That dear boy is standing in my front yard, getting handsomer right before my eyes!" Her grandmother was clearly picking up steam. "I swear, he looks even better than he did a few minutes ago. If you don't hurry, half the women in Ryder's County are going to beat you to him!"

In the mirror behind the shelves, Marnie inspected herself. Why had she worn this country-style flowered skirt and peasant blouse? Tom had become a man of the world. She didn't want him to think she'd turned into a hick.

"I promise I'll get there as soon as I can, but I need to drop by my house first."

"Oh, take as long as you like!" replied her grandmother. "Who cares if my blood pressure is going off the charts?"

Marnie was by nature easygoing, but she could be pushed only so far. Besides, having lived under her grandmother's supervision from the age of ten until her marriage, she knew the older woman's capacity for histrionics.

"Now look, *Jolene*." She spoke her first name with emphasis, which they both knew meant she'd reached her limit. "I will get there when I get there."

There came a short and—to her experienced ears, disgruntled—silence. Then her grandmother said, "Well, I'm not going to quarrel two days before Christmas. You will be here for dinner tonight, won't you?"

"Since I'm cooking it, I most certainly will. Now go take your medicine and call Dr. Spindler if you're feeling bad, although I wish you'd let me take you to a specialist in Nashville."

"He's been my doctor for fifty years, and he's good enough for me," Jolene said with admirable steadiness for someone in such precarious health. "He delivered my two children, and he'll bury me. That's the way I want it."

"See you later," Marnie said. "I love you."

After ringing off, she made a quick tour of the store, straightening the jackets on the bestsellers and adjusting the half-price sign on a rack of calendars. Other than that, everything was in its customary ship-shape.

Following her divorce, Marnie had returned to Tennessee and used the small inheritance left by her parents to buy the town's bookstore. As Ryder's Crossing grew, she'd also bought the store next to it and expanded both her floor space and her selection of merchandise.

Although she had to compete with mail order and the Internet, not to mention her customers' shopping trips to Nashville, forty miles away, Marnie had done well. People appreciated her personal service and large stock, the homey touches and the offbeat items she hunted down at trade shows.

She wondered what Tom would think of the place—not that she expected him to visit it. He'd come home for Christmas to see her grandmother, not his ex-wife. The man Marnie had loved since high school was virtually a stranger now.

She locked the receipts in the safe and switched on the automatic answering machine. Tomorrow and Christmas Eve, she could trust Betty to run the store. Although Marnie thought of herself as indispensable, she knew her friend was reliable and efficient.

After pulling on her jacket, she locked the front door and exited through the rear. A chill December wind nipped her cheeks, and she could feel a tang in the air that hinted at snow.

Across the alley behind the store lay a charming, old-fashioned neighborhood of redbrick houses and well-kept yards. Marnie had been lucky enough to buy the property directly behind her shop, a two-story home that dated from the thirties.

It was the kind of place she'd dreamed of someday sharing with Tom. Who could have imagined that, at age thirty-two, she would be living here alone and childless, while Tom worked in Rome?

She knew his childhood had been difficult, with an alcoholic father and a mother who had abandoned him. As a teenager, after he and Marnie became friends, he'd accepted Granny's offer to move in with them and help on the farm while he finished high school.

While attending the University of Tennessee in Knoxville together, they'd fallen in love. Or, at least, Marnie had.

They'd managed, with difficulty, to refrain from making love until they were married. Then the experience, the first for them both, had been explosive and delirious.

She'd gladly shared Tom's life as he joined the Foreign Service, trained in Washington, and was posted to Tokyo and then Stockholm. Their lovemaking had been wonderful, and they'd both enjoyed exploring new places and cultures. For a while she'd believed their marriage was perfect.

But after four years she'd broached the subject of children. Tom's response had stunned her: absolutely and definitely no. He didn't want them and he never would.

It had taken her another two years to accept the fact that she would never change his mind. Tom wanted a companion, not a wife to build a family with. Marnie's deep yearning for children only made him resentful, and she was afraid that, if she didn't make a break, they might grow to hate each other.

So she had come back to Tennessee and had gotten a divorce. She just wished it were that easy to fall out of love and to find someone new. Four years had passed, and she hadn't met anyone who came close to taking Tom's place.

He was still single, too, but she couldn't read anything into that. He had always been a loner.

Marnie let herself into the house and hurried across polished wooden floors, past antique furniture that she'd bought from the previous owners. Stuffed bears, her own contribution, peeked at her from tables and shelves.

She'd been lucky to find a place already in prime condition, the floors refinished and the kitchen updated. The owners had been moving out of state and planned to rent for a while, so they'd sold most of their larger items to save shipping and storage.

Marnie had added her own personal touches—photographs and books as well as the bears. The result was an appealing coziness that lacked only the chirp of little voices and the firmness of masculine footsteps to make it complete.

Upstairs she tried on a suit and a tailored dress before switching back to her skirt and blouse. Why should she try to impress Tom with her sophistication? He knew she was a country girl. He'd been a country boy himself, not long ago.

She collected a shopping bag full of gifts for Granny, Tom, her aunt and uncle, and their estranged son, her cousin Mike. He was driving in from Santa Fe for a long-delayed reunion.

In the kitchen Marnie took out the zucchini lasagna she'd prepared in advance. With French bread and a salad, it should make a meal that even a world traveler couldn't look down his nose at.

Everything fit easily into the back of her station wagon, along with her small suitcase. At Jolene's urging, Marnie had agreed to stay at the farmhouse for a four-day weekend.

Although it was only five miles from town, snow could make the road hazardous. Besides, there was no substitute for waking up in her childhood bed on Christmas morning and coming downstairs to join the family.

And Tom would be there, Marnie thought with a twist of bittersweet longing. He wasn't family anymore, but they could at least be friends again.

This time, she decided as she backed out of the driveway, she would view him objectively. She wouldn't fool herself into mistaking his affection for love. It wasn't fair to either of them.

Outside of town Marnie crossed a wooden bridge over the creek and followed the curving road through a copse of trees. *Over the river and through the woods to Grandmother's house we go,* she thought.

A few miles later the trees thinned, yielding glimpses of rolling farmland. Grazing cows dotted brownish fields, which in summer would turn as green as Oz.

She spotted her grandmother's mailbox in the twilight, made to resemble a birdhouse. Years ago someone had left the door open after collecting the mail, and a bird had actually nested in it. Her grandfather had put up a temporary mailbox until the fledglings flew away.

The station wagon swung into the driveway. Before her sprawled a landscape that Marnie knew in all its moods, from the duck pond around one side to the dormant kitchen garden marked by withered cornstalks. The farmland in back was rented to a neighbor, who kept the premises in good repair as part of the arrangement.

A three-story gray clapboard farmhouse and a weathered barn dominated the setting. There was nothing fancy about the house; even the shutters were painted the same unassuming gray. Yet, to Marnie, the solid, reassuring structure reflected the fact that generations of Aftons had lived here in peace and modest comfort.

A light-blue rental car sat to one side of the carport, leaving room inside for Marnie's station wagon next to Granny's sedan.

She parked and was opening the rear hatch when she felt a change in the air. She knew it was Tom, without being aware that she'd heard his footsteps or caught a whiff of his aftershave.

The hairs prickled along her arms, beneath her quilted jacket. Forcing herself to smile, Marnie turned to greet her former husband.

At the edge of the carport Tom stood watching her, his lips slightly parted, his eyes questioning. There wasn't a hint of the sophisticate about him today. It was as if he'd reverted to his old self the moment he set foot back in Tennessee.

Despite his tapered hairstyle, a blond lock fell rakishly onto his forehead. A woodsman's jacket and jeans highlighted the tautness of his body.

She knew that broad chest and those slim hips and muscular thighs. She had measured every inch of him with her own body, many times.

At the sight of him Marnie felt her breasts ripen and warmth ignite below the curve of her stomach. It was as if her body had slept for four years, and now he had brought it back to life.

She heard the swift, indrawn breath that marked his own response. Their chemistry remained as potent as ever, Marnie realized. But this time she wouldn't mistake it for love.

"You cut your hair," he said.

"It got in the way." Instinctively she touched her shoulder-length hair. She used to wear her thick, brown tresses nearly to her waist, but she'd trimmed it since the divorce. "How about helping me carry this stuff in?"

"I thought we should talk privately for a few minutes first." He cocked his head, an old, endearing habit that meant he was uncertain of how she might respond.

Like the shy teenager she'd been when they first met, Marnie wanted to avert her gaze and scurry away. But she stood her ground. "All right. So, how are you?"

"Fine." He started to say more, then fell silent. Tom spoke three languages and had won a debate trophy in college. He rarely became tongue-tied.

Searching for a topic, Marnie said, "That must have been exciting last summer, when you went to Malta." He'd helped provide staff assistance at an economic conference.

"Granny told you about it?"

"It was in the paper," she said.

"Really? I'm surprised." His breath made a cloud in the crisp air. "I didn't know the local bigwigs were aware of my existence."

"You're one of Ryder High's most distinguished

graduates.'' Marnie meant every word, but Tom gave a dismissive shake of the head, as if she must be joking.

"How's the store?" he asked.

"I make a living." After paying herself a salary, Marnie reinvested the small profit. "Anyway, I know Granny appreciates your coming home. She's been talking about it for weeks."

"How could I not come back?" His brow furrowed. "When she told me this might be her last Christmas, I made the reservations that same day."

"She said that?" Marnie stared at him in dismay.

"Surely you knew!"

"She complains about her heart, but she's been doing that for years." Guilt coursed through her. She should have paid closer attention.

"Well, she told me it's getting worse," Tom said grimly. "She doesn't expect to last another year."

Marnie wrapped her arms around herself and felt the tears sting. She didn't want to cry in front of Tom, not for any reason, so she hurried on. "No wonder my aunt and uncle are flying in from Chicago." Usually her uncle, a minister, spent the holidays conducting Christmas services at his church.

"Haven't you heard?" Tom moved closer, filling her senses with a masculine aroma that was part aftershave and part subliminal allure. "O'Hare Airport's closed due to snow. We're hoping it'll reopen tomorrow."

"I hope they can make it." Marnie hadn't thought to check out-of-state weather. "Are the roads bad from Santa Fe? My cousin Mike is driving in."

"Not that I know of." As he reached past her for

the suitcase and the bag of gifts, Tom brushed against Marnie. A wave of fire swept over her skin, but if he felt anything, he hid it well. All he said was, "Playing Santa? Those are a lot of gifts."

"I run a shop, remember?" She fought to keep her tone casual. "Besides, I'm sure you picked up plenty of trinkets on your travels."

"A few." He paused, so close she could almost taste him. His body curved over hers, creating a private space for the two of them, and his lids drifted down seductively.

He was going to kiss her. Marnie couldn't stop him, and she didn't want to.

Without warning, he straightened and yanked her luggage from the car. "I don't want to mislead you, Marnie. Things aren't simple anymore."

His rejection reverberated like a slap. "They never were." She lifted out the casserole and the plastic bag of bread and salad fixings. "But then, I'm not the girl I used to be. I've been on my own for four years now."

"You don't have to remind me," he muttered.

"It's getting cold." The wind had picked up, but the chill that ran through Marnie had nothing to do with the weather. "Let's go inside."

"I want to explain—"

"It can wait," she said, and, yielding to impulse, fled toward the house.

IT HADN'T BEEN TOM'S intention to stand there gawking. Yet, despite his years as a diplomat, he felt clumsy around Marnie and afraid of saying the wrong thing.

This thrumming in his body, this tightening need—he'd been free of it for a long time, but it came roaring back the minute he saw her. When he got close, he felt as if she were touching him in places that still, in spite of everything, belonged to her.

It didn't help to realize that, unintentionally, he'd betrayed her. He wanted to prepare her, but the right words escaped him. Maybe there were no right words.

The first time he'd noticed her had been their freshman year in high school. He'd been walking down the hall when he spotted her at a locker. He'd stumbled and dropped his books like a stupid kid.

She'd shot him a startled look and scampered off to class. It had taken Tom months to work up the nerve to talk to her, but as soon as he did, he discovered a soul mate.

It was because of her that he'd gone out for the high school gymnastics team, so he could show off in front of Marnie like some primitive male. Even after he moved in with her and her grandmother, he'd never lost that sense of awe in her presence, as if something rare and wonderful had dropped magically into his life.

When she left him, when he realized she didn't love him enough to accept him completely, it had been even worse than when his mother had deserted his father and him. Tom had discovered long ago that he could survive almost anything, but this had been the bitterest pill of all.

Even now, he ached to catch her in his arms and try again to make things right. But they couldn't. In his struggle to regain control of his life, he'd unwittingly destroyed any hope of reconciliation.

Ahead of him Marnie climbed the porch steps and opened the door. Suddenly Tom realized that he should have gone in first.

''Hold on!'' Following her, he had to angle sideways through the door to accommodate the packages. ''There's something—''

Marnie stopped so suddenly he nearly ran into her. Gazing over her head, he spotted little Cody trotting out of Jolene's bedroom.

The blond boy regarded Marnie with interest. ''Hi!''

Tom caught his breath. He doubted he could have spoken if his life depended on it.

''Who are you?'' She sounded amused and puzzled as she greeted the child.

''I'm Cody.''

''Well, I'm Marnie. And if you'll let me put this stuff in the kitchen, I'd be happy to shake hands with you.'' She skirted the child carefully. ''Where's your mommy? Are your folks new in the area?''

''I don't have a mommy,'' the little boy chirped, and ran to Tom. ''This is my daddy!''

Chapter Two

Marnie couldn't have heard the little boy correctly. "What did you say?"

"Daddy!" The child pointed for emphasis. A ray of sunlight turned his ash-blond hair nearly white, but his eyes remained a much-too-familiar shade of clear blue.

"I wanted to tell you, but I didn't know how." Tom stood behind her, his breath warm against her neck. "I wrote Granny six months ago, but I guess she wasn't any better at finding the words than I was."

A child. Tom had a child.

Numbly, Marnie stared down at the moppet. Although his hair was lighter than her ex-husband's, there was no denying the resemblance.

How was it possible? They'd only been divorced for four years, and she guessed Cody to be about two and a half. Tom must have found another woman soon after she left.

It was possible he'd fallen for a woman on the rebound, but Marnie refused to fool herself. She'd known all along that he would want children when he found the right mate.

No wonder Granny hadn't mentioned anything. It hurt like fire to know that the man she loved had so easily found happiness with someone else.

Still, it was cruel of him to spring it on her this way! Her voice trembling, Marnie said, "I don't see what's so difficult about sending a wedding announcement."

"I'm not married," he murmured as his son padded down the hall ahead of them, toward the kitchen.

"My, you have changed." She wanted to focus on anything but her own sharp sense of loss. "You didn't used to believe in having children out of wedlock. Unless it's your...your girlfriend who doesn't believe in marriage."

"There is no girlfriend." Tom shoved his hands into his pockets, more like the teenager she remembered than the man he'd become. "It was an accident."

Marnie refused to acknowledge a sneaking sense of relief. Instead, she reminded herself that accidents didn't just happen, especially not to grown men who had managed to remain childless through six years of marriage. "Sort of like getting hit by a truck?"

"I got careless," Tom said. "Believe me, I didn't do it deliberately."

Despite the look of remorse on his face, Marnie wanted to lash out, however irrationally. "He is a sweet little boy. Don't talk about him as if he were a...a stray kitten!" She stalked into the kitchen in Cody's wake.

The room, which stretched along the back of the

house, was lined with modernized counters, cabinets and appliances. Through the large windows, she could see willow rockers sitting on the screened porch and, in the yard, a rose garden, pruned for the winter. Farther away stretched the sleeping fields.

There was no sign of Jolene. "Where's Granny?"

Tom reached the doorway. "Resting."

"She didn't sound very restful when she called me half an hour ago to hurry me up!" Marnie challenged.

"Okay, she's not resting, she's hiding," Tom said. "In her bedroom. Want to make a federal case of it?"

She smacked the casserole onto the tile counter and went to preheat the oven. Just before he'd passed away, Grandpa Ewell had done a good job of remodeling the room, but he hadn't provided enough floor space, especially not for her and a man she wished were standing somewhere in the next county, or maybe the next solar system.

"Can I have some *vino?*" Cody asked.

"What?" Marnie swung around in amazement. "You give this child wine?"

"We do live in Italy." Amusement lit Tom's eyes.

"That's reprehensible! It's…it's unthinkable!" she sputtered.

"Calm down." He moved past her and opened the refrigerator. "*Vino* is what we call grape juice in our household." He took out a bottle of purple juice labeled for children.

"*Vino* is Italian for wine!" Marnie knew that much about the language. "You're teaching him bad habits. Just wait till my uncle gets here!" A minister, Norbert Galloway adhered to old-fashioned morality.

"What's your uncle Norbert going to do to me?"

Tom asked mildly. He poured the juice into a plastic cup and handed it to his son.

"*Grazie.*" Cody walked with a swinging gait to the small breakfast table. He even moved like his father, Marnie thought with a pang.

"Never mind my uncle." It had been a foolish threat, anyway. "I just meant you should always strive to set a good example." She tore the foil from the casserole so hard she ripped it. "Kids are impressionable. Everything you do or say has an effect."

Tom leaned against the counter and watched her slide the baking dish into the oven. "My own parents weren't good role models, so I find myself winging it. Olivia says I'm not much better than a *ragazzaccio,* a naughty boy, myself."

Olivia. The beautiful name brought home the reality of this other woman, Cody's mother. She might not be Tom's girlfriend any longer, but the two of them would be linked forever by this little boy. "I suppose she's very attractive."

"Who?"

"Olivia." Marnie opened the bag of prepared salad greens and dumped them into a bowl, then set to work slicing tomatoes.

"Actually, she's kind of heavy." From a cabinet, Tom fetched a cookie sheet for toasting the bread.

"Lots of women have trouble losing weight after childbearing." Marnie didn't exactly want to hear him rave about Cody's mother, but a man ought to respect the mother of his own child.

"It's been nearly thirty years since Olivia gave birth." Tom was chuckling now. "I think she owes

her weight to fettuccine Alfredo and *pasticcini*—
that's baked goods.''

"Nonna Olivia mi ama," Cody chimed in from the
table.

"That means, 'Grandma Olivia loves me,''' Tom
explained. "She isn't really his grandmother, of
course. She's my housekeeper."

"Oh." Marnie felt her cheeks flaming. "Well, is it
a big secret, or are you going to tell me who his
mother is?''

"Not in front of him. That would be indiscreet, and
I'm trying to set a good example for my son, remember?'' Tom quirked one eyebrow.

Ragazzaccio, Marnie thought. Naughty boy. He
certainly looked like one at the moment.

None of Tom's story made sense, none of it fit the
man she knew. An accident? This man paid close attention to the smallest detail in his life and his work.

At least he'd taken the boy in and obviously loved
him. One part of Marnie's spirit applauded her ex-
husband's responsibility and kindness. The other part
wanted to throw something at him.

She yearned with every part of her being to have
a child. A bright-eyed baby, smelling of talcum pow-
der and milk, to hold in her arms; or a little boy like
this one, with chubby hands and a vivacious smile.
And a husband to gaze lovingly at the two of them.

She would have given almost anything, gone almost anywhere with Tom, to make such joy possible.
Now the years were passing, and her arms were
empty.

It would serve him right if she upended the salad
bowl over his arrogant head. Unfortunately, he knew

her well enough to shift out of reach whenever she moved in his direction. Maybe the fact that she was vigorously cutting tomatoes had something to do with his skittishness, she admitted silently.

"Well?" he said finally.

"Well, what?"

"Are you going to carve me up with that knife, or forgive me?"

Forgive him? Marnie knew it was her moral duty not to hold grudges, but...

She would have to learn to live with this turn of events, even though it felt like a betrayal. Certainly the little boy drinking juice at the table deserved nothing but tenderness.

But how could she forgive Tom, when it hurt to see how happy he was, having a child without her? That was more than Marnie could manage.

"You're still alive," she said. "Don't push your luck."

His laughter rippled through the air. It had been such a rare sound years ago that it couldn't help giving her pleasure, even now.

She remembered how bedraggled he'd looked that rainy, autumn evening when a sixteen-year-old Tom had knocked at the back door. He'd quarreled with his drunken father, who'd thrown him out.

His wet clothes were stuck to his too-thin frame, and there was desperation on his face. He had nowhere to go, so he'd come to see Marnie, his best friend.

Grandpa Ewell had died the previous year. Despite their efforts to bolster each other, the teenage Marnie and the then sixty-two-year-old Jolene had rattled around the house like a pair of leftover bolts in an empty truck.

Granny had taken one look at Tom and hauled him inside. She'd clucked and fussed, clearly dismayed by his father's cruelty.

Although Granny didn't know Tom well, she'd appreciated the way he dropped by occasionally, volunteering to do chores without expecting any payment. Whenever he was invited to stay for dinner, he beamed as if he were being handed a golden ticket to Paradise.

And so, that rainy autumn night, Granny asked him to stay with them in exchange for helping around the farm. Tom leaped at the chance.

His presence illuminated the house. Cold, dark spaces turned warm again. His laughter, his vitality and his joy at finding a home were exactly what the two women needed.

And still needed, Marnie thought wistfully. But she would have to find them with another man, because this one was no longer hers.

She finished tossing the salad and noted that the casserole wouldn't be done for half an hour. "I'm going to see Granny."

She meant that as a cue for Tom to leave her alone, but he refused to take a hint. "Great! I want to spend as much time with her as possible."

His words reminded Marnie that her grandmother was, apparently, in worse shape than she'd realized. "If she feels so poorly, we shouldn't all jam in there at once."

"A crowd might cheer her up," Tom said with mock innocence.

"Are you deliberately contradicting everything I say?"

"Who, me?"

"Well, let's not fight in front of her, all right?" Marnie said.

"I'm not the one who insists on fighting." Tom's low, suggestive tone made her pulse speed up. Marnie turned quickly away.

"Don't fight," Cody added from the table. "Be friends!"

"A future diplomat." Tom collected his son's empty cup and lifted the toddler from his chair.

As he raised the giggling boy overhead, the two formed such a perfect picture that Marnie wished she could capture it on film. The father, tall and powerful, was completely enraptured; the son, exhilarated at his distance from the floor, remained secure in his daddy's love.

This was how she'd imagined things would be when she and Tom had a family. It seemed so natural, so perfect, that she couldn't resent the fact that this was not her child. She was glad Tom had discovered, one way or another, the joys of parenthood.

Had he changed in other ways? she wondered. Until she knew more about his relationship with Cody's mother, she couldn't begin to understand the man that he'd become.

In the meantime, she did not want him to hear her conversation with Jolene. "I'll peek in first to make sure Granny's not sleeping," Marnie said. "You two can play for a while."

Without waiting for a response, she hurried out of the kitchen. She needed to sort out the impressions buzzing through her head. The shocking discovery that Tom had a son. The disturbing realization that she wanted him as much as ever, but that he had turned to someone else.

Her grandmother had always been Tom's ardent supporter, so Marnie didn't expect objectivity. Still, no one knew him, or her, better than this strong-minded lady who had raised Marnie since the age of ten.

After Marnie and Tom's wedding, Jolene had moved downstairs, taking over a large room in the front corner of the house. Formerly her grandfather's office, it had served as Tom's room during his teenage years.

The window offered a view of comings and goings in the yard. In addition, it was conveniently located next to the front entrance hall, near the bottom of the stairs and across from the living room. A perfect command post, except that with everyone gone there had been no one to command for years now.

That had changed for the weekend, Marnie reflected. Heart troubles or not, Granny must relish the return, however temporarily, to the days when she ruled the roost.

She tapped at the door and heard a scuffling as if someone were moving inside. After a moment, Jolene's quavery voice called, ''Come in!''

Marnie peeked in. In the quilt-covered double bed lay her grandmother, her white hair fluffed across the pillow. Her skin had a bright, healthy color, however, and she was breathing fast for someone who had been resting.

Jolene's face reflected her strong character: a prom-

inent, rounded nose that Grandpa used to call bump-
tious; an expressive mouth that had thinned only a
little since its rosebud youth; and cheeks sprinkled
with freckles.

Could she really be so ill? Only last weekend she'd
driven into town with Dr. Spindler, who lived nearby.
After church she'd eaten lunch at Marnie's house and
chatted as merrily as ever, although she *had* complained about feeling weak.

Marnie's gaze searched for any hallmark of serious
illness: pill bottles on the bedside table, breathing
equipment, a walker. All she spotted was the mahog-
any cane that had been her grandpa's during his final
illness, and which Jolene used more for poking stray
dogs out of her path than for support.

As for the bedside table, it was occupied by a par-
tially filled-in Scrabble board. Then Marnie noticed
something new atop the corner desk: a computer.
"When did you get this?"

"Oh, the Ryans picked it up for me in Nashville a
while back." Granny waved one liver-spotted hand
vaguely, as if it were the most natural thing in the
world for her next-door neighbors to "pick up" a
computer for her.

"Why?" Marnie approached the bed.

"What a silly question!" Granny heaved a sigh, as
if from the depths of exhaustion. "Everybody has a
computer these days. How else can I do my taxes?"

Perching on the edge of the bed, Marnie leaned to
kiss her grandmother's dry cheek. Expensive French
cologne wafted up. "You smell wonderful. Is that for
me, or Tom?"

"Oh, all of you. And Artie—Doc Spindler dropped

by earlier.'' She reached up to tuck a stray lock of Marnie's hair behind her ear. ''I don't know why you ever cut your hair. You used to be able to wind it into such a nice French twist. It made you look like Audrey Hepburn.''

Marnie didn't think she bore the least resemblance to her grandmother's favorite actress, but she knew better than to squabble. Instead, she went to the heart of what was bothering her. ''Why didn't you tell me Tom had a child?''

Jolene stopped fussing with Marnie's hair. ''I know I should have. Just call me an old coward.''

''What on earth were you afraid of?''

''Hurting you,'' her grandmother admitted. ''For a while, I was tempted to fly to Rome and strangle that man. Of course, I'm too frail for that. So I decided it was his duty to come here and let you strangle him yourself.''

The reference to being frail reminded Marnie about her grandmother's health. ''Are you really that ill? You told Tom you were practically dying.''

Jolene poked at a loose thread on the quilt. ''This *could* be my last Christmas. You know I'm not well.''

''You've got to let me take you into Nashville to see a specialist!'' The only response was a fierce glare. ''Oh, let me do something! I love you so much.''

''And I love you.'' Jolene stroked her arm. ''Maybe seeing all my family around me again will help me rally. You never know.''

''I certainly hope so.'' Marnie suspected Jolene was deliberately putting her off, but was she exaggerating the extent of her illness, or minimizing it?

Through the partly open door trotted Cody, his little face alight and his busy feet stumbling in their haste. "Can I play more 'puter, Nonna Jola?"

"Nonna Jola?" Marnie raised an eyebrow skeptically.

"We decided it would be a suitable name for Cody to call me," her grandmother replied. "Cody, I'd rather you didn't—"

Too late. The little boy bounded to the desk and poked a key. Immediately the blank screen was invaded by hopping, squeaking gremlins.

"You bought a computer game?" Marnie asked. "Why on earth?"

"It came with the system," her grandmother said. "I have no idea how these things work."

"But, Nonna Jola! You beat me, 'member?"

Tom followed his son into the room, a cellular phone pressed to his ear. After a moment he punched a button and put the phone in his pocket. "No change in Chicago. They've canceled all flights out of O'Hare. Looks like Uncle Norbert isn't going to get a chance to cure me of my evil ways."

"What?" Granny glared at Cody, who had begun shooting down gremlins. "Look here, boy, you're missing half of them! If you're going to play, do it right! Now, what's this about evil?"

"Uncle Norbert doesn't approve of having kids out of wedlock," Marnie said weakly. She wished she'd never brought up the subject in the first place. "Not that I think he's going to chastise Tom in front of everyone."

"He'd better not. Especially when he finds out what his own son's done." Granny clapped her hand over her mouth. Between her fingers, she told Marnie, "Forget I said anything."

"Jolene, what *else* are you up to?" she demanded. Apparently the planned reconciliation between Cousin Mike and his parents wasn't going to be a simple matter, either. "If there are any more surprises, maybe you'd better tell me right now, so I don't keep tripping over them."

Tom's chuckle stopped her.

"What is it, young man?" Jolene demanded. "I fail to find any mirth in my daughter and son-in-law being stuck in Chicago in a snowstorm!"

"Yes, but you and Marnie squabble about everything so delightfully. I've missed you more than I can say." He beamed at the women, and at his son, absorbed in the game. "Things are never dull around here."

Thank goodness, Marnie thought. Because even sitting here between her grandmother and a two-year-old, she couldn't stop studying Tom's strong shoulders and the impish gleam on his face and the masculine way he held himself.

She wanted as much tumult and interruption as her grandmother could manage. Anything to keep her from being alone with Tom.

There'd been a few men she'd dated occasionally over the years, taking her to movies and dancing, wanting to hold her. She'd never felt a tenth as excited being kissed good-night by any of them as she felt just looking at Tom.

He made her scalp tingle and her cheeks flush, and her body want to yield beneath his touch. The iron will that had held her world together for the past four years was melting merely from being in the same room with him.

The phone on Jolene's end table rang. A thin, spotted hand clamped onto it before Marnie could move. "Let's hope that's good news from your uncle or your cousin!"

But it wasn't, she could tell from her grandmother's end of the conversation. She heard, "Mike! Where are you?" and "Really?" and "There must be a garage open somewhere!" and "I don't know why they can't make all the parts interchangeable so you could carry one in the trunk and not have to go hunting for a—what is it?—water pump, two days before Christmas!"

When she rang off, she said, "Mike's car broke down near Memphis."

Near Memphis. That meant her cousin wouldn't be arriving until tomorrow.

The uncomfortable truth dawned on Marnie. She couldn't count on any of her relatives arriving to serve as a buffer.

She was stuck with Tom. They were going to have to work together to make Granny's last Christmas wonderful and joyous and special.

She hoped they wouldn't kill each other in the process.

Chapter Three

Tom wouldn't wish a mechanical breakdown on anyone, but he was glad Mike had been delayed. He was even happier that Marnie's stern old uncle Norbert wasn't bearing down on him.

He wanted as much time alone with Marnie as he could get. Not that he believed anything would change between them. After all, she'd never fully accepted him, and the unexpected appearance of Cody would probably worsen the situation.

But he wanted to be with her. He kept getting lost in those expressive brown eyes of hers, with the way every emotion wrote itself plainly across her face—dismay and delight, warmth and uncertainty.

Spending time with Marnie, for minutes and sometimes hours at a time, had pulled Tom from his teenage fog of anger and boredom. Through her he'd learned the excitement of studying about faraway places and ancient times; he'd experienced the soul-stirring power of poetry; he'd come awake to the possibilities of his own mind.

He hadn't thought in terms of boyfriend-girlfriend or love, not back then, although he experienced mighty surges of adolescent lust. He'd reined it in ruthlessly, valuing Marnie's friendship too much to risk it.

They'd both changed a lot since those days. Four years ago her rejection had been so painful that Tom had wondered for a time how he would survive. Cody had brought him back, even though he knew Cody might also destroy any chance of reconciliation with her.

Tom couldn't worry about that now. In his work he organized the present and planned for the future. But this Christmas existed as an island in time.

He intended to live it moment to moment, relishing the glow of Marnie's skin and the vulnerability of her smile. From an early age he had armored himself against the world, but he'd never been able to shut her out, and he didn't want to. However much it might hurt, he would take what he could get, gladly.

Trying to keep his voice light, he said, "It appears you and I are in charge of Christmas this year."

"I'm afraid so." Jolene sank into the pillow. The flowers embroidered on the case winked as if ruffled by a spring breeze. "It'll be up to you two to handle the decorating, not to mention cooking the turkey."

"Cooking!" Marnie jumped to her feet. "The casserole should have been out five minutes ago!"

"Need any help?" With a wink at Jolene, Tom followed. To no one's surprise, Cody stayed glued to the computer screen.

In the kitchen Marnie stuck her hands into two quilted mitts, retrieved the glass baking dish and set it atop the unlit burners to cool. The bubbly cheese had turned dark brown around the edges, but there was no serious damage.

Tom closed the oven door. "I can burn the bread for you, too, if you like," he teased.

"I can handle it." Keeping her back to him, Marnie moved along the counter to the long, thin loaves of bread. "Would you look in the cabinet for some garlic salt?"

He couldn't help himself. "Marnie, turn around and face me."

"I will not!"

So she was deliberately shutting him out. If only he were better at judging her emotions by her tone of voice! Tom couldn't tell if she were merely snappish, or hurting, too.

She'd walked out on him without a backward glance, and since then sent him nothing but cold, official communications via her lawyer. But she had to feel something.

"You told me when you left that we weren't suited to each other," he said. "That we'd made a mistake."

"That's right." Her voice sounded brittle, almost shrill.

"Then why are you angry with me?"

"I'm not!" She sliced the loaves in half lengthwise and slathered them with butter.

"Then who are you mad at? The cookie sheet?"

"The weather in Chicago!" she rasped. "Granny's heart! And Mike's car for breaking down!"

The peasant blouse was cut low enough in back for Tom to see the soft indentation along her spine, below the swinging brown hair. He knew she would shudder if he trailed kisses down to the cotton fabric. On second thought, she might decide to butter *him,* so he refrained.

As she stood in profile, he noticed a pearl nestled in her earlobe like a polished extension of her own flesh. He couldn't resist rubbing his forefinger over it.

She drew back. "What are you doing?"

He dropped his hand, but ignored the question. Instead he said, "You're angry about a lot of things, aren't you? I've learned that when people offer too many explanations, they're withholding the real one."

"You can't figure out why I want to pummel you into a heap?" Cookie sheet in hand, she moved toward the oven so abruptly that if Tom hadn't dodged, he would have received an elbow in the midsection. "Your son shouldn't be separated from his mother at Christmas. You should have brought her, too."

"I can't," Tom said. "She's dead."

He saw her flinch. There was a pause before she said, "I'm sorry."

"An aneurysm." He didn't know why he kept talking, except to fill the silence. "She was only thirty."

As Marnie straightened after putting the bread in the oven, he saw that she was holding back tears. "That's terrible. You must miss her very much."

"I hardly knew her." Tom supposed it reflected badly on him, but he wouldn't lie about it.

He remembered Elise as a sweet-tempered young woman with broad Swedish cheekbones. At the men's shop where she worked she'd worn her blond braids piled atop her head, and even in bed she'd taken them down but hadn't brushed out her hair. Too much trouble to fix it again, he supposed.

"Then why—" Marnie jerked open the silverware drawer and removed cutlery for dinner. "Never mind. It's none of my business."

"Go ahead, ask." He waited, unwilling to volunteer any more. When Marnie was upset, she always tried to hide her emotions. Well, Tom didn't intend to satisfy her curiosity unless she broke down and asked about Elise.

Maybe that was unfair; after all, he wasn't always forthcoming about his own feelings, either. But Marnie was the one who'd refused to accept him the way he was.

She'd escaped back to this town, where she belonged and Tom never would. He wanted to know that she cared enough to let down her guard. That she'd missed him, at least a little. That she wasn't merely angry because he'd deprived her of the children she wanted.

Oh, heck, he didn't know what he expected from her. He certainly wasn't going to get what he wanted. Partial love, conditional love, could never be enough, and that was the only thing Marnie had ever given him.

"I'm sure you wrote the whole story to Granny." She busied herself setting the kitchen table.

"Part of it." Tom fetched glasses and filled them with water. They weren't childproof, but he'd noticed that Cody was rapidly gaining in dexterity.

Although Nonna Olivia handled most of the cooking and child care, Tom tried hard to be a hands-on father. Maybe he boiled pasta to the point of doughiness and made a clumsy horsey, lumbering around the living room of their large apartment, but he could tell Cody enjoyed his efforts. And he loved watching his son develop day by day.

The boy was an unexpected treasure. But the greatest treasure, the one Tom had wanted since his teenage years, stood right in front of him.

Marnie bustled by him, laying down paper napkins. The temptation to reach out was irresistible. From behind he slid his hands around her waist. She went stock-still.

Marnie was, as he remembered, slender but soft. Her petite figure had curves that made him ache to run his hands higher and cup her breasts.

She remained standing there, apparently unaware that she was crumpling the napkins in her hand. Cautiously, not wanting to set off her defense alarms, Tom turned her around and brushed a strand of hair from her cheek.

Near panic showed in her expression, but then it eased. Her gaze grew soft and her lips parted, as if preparing for his kiss.

Tom wasn't about to disappoint a lady.

MARNIE COULDN'T THINK about anything except the way Tom was standing so close, his palm touching her cheek, his eyes as warm as a summer sky.

His mouth came down on hers. She knew she shouldn't let him, but she needed this.

Needed to touch his shoulder and feel the hard muscle flex beneath her hand. To lick the inner edges of his lips and hear his responsive rasp of breathing.

Soon he and Cody would go off to their faraway land, to their life without her. So how could it hurt to wrap her arms around his neck and meet his kiss halfway? It was a memory that she could keep when he was gone.

Marnie had suppressed her feelings for Tom so long that they surprised her with their power and sweetness. She had forgotten that love was not only aching disappointment—it was also joy.

She wasn't sure who regained self-control first, but they knew each other so well that the other picked up the subtle withdrawal instantly. Tom nuzzled her hair one last time before drawing away. "That felt good for me. And you, too, I think."

She couldn't deny it. "Yes. But that's as far as it goes."

"Are you sure?" There were shadows in his eyes. "Maybe it's time to heal old wounds. Marnie, we had something precious between us. I don't want to lose it."

"It's a bit late for regrets, wouldn't you say?" Swallowing hard, she extracted herself from his arms and did her best to straighten the wrinkled napkins as she folded them on the table.

He regarded her ruefully. "You're still not going to ask me, are you?"

"Ask you what?" She knew perfectly well, but she refused to yield another inch.

Marnie had thrown her pride away before. She'd urged Tom to reconsider his position on children, offered to wait a few years if that would help, and done her best to explain how deep her maternal instinct ran.

Her pleading had, if anything, backfired. The more she pursued the subject, the more he withdrew. They'd reached the point where the atmosphere in their Stockholm apartment became so chilly it was intolerable.

Well, someone had thawed him, and not long after Marnie had departed. Someone else had lit Tom's fire through the long Swedish winter.

Clamping her lips together, she hurried to retrieve the bread. "I guess everything's ready." She transferred the half loaves onto a serving dish.

"Marnie, stop this." Tom planted himself in front of her. "You want to know about Elise, so stop torturing yourself. Let me tell you."

She guessed that he had lost an inner battle to wait until she begged for answers. The least she could do was make a concession in return. "Okay. Frankly, I'm dying to know."

He touched his forehead to hers, creating a private space between them. "Thank you."

"For what?"

"Admitting that."

"It wasn't easy."

"We're both stubborn, aren't we?" he said.

"Nearly as mule-headed as my grandmother," she agreed.

"As bad as that?"

They both chuckled. Marnie's tension eased, and she let Tom steer her into a chair.

"After you left..." He cleared his throat before going on. "I met a saleslady in a shop. Elise was flirtatious and lighthearted. She assured me she wasn't seeking a serious involvement."

"What did she look like?" Now that he'd started, Marnie intended to satisfy her curiosity to the fullest.

"Blond hair in braids. Gray eyes."

"Milkmaid type? Or sultry?"

"In between."

"There's no such thing!" she flared. "I want specifics."

His mouth twisted puckishly. "Height, weight, glove size?"

"You can skip the glove size."

"Taller than you, heavier than you, nothing like you in any way. I wasn't in the market for an imitation," he said.

Marnie wasn't sure how to take that remark. The truth, she reflected wryly, was rarely as neat as one might wish. "Ugly?" she asked hopefully. "Oh, never mind."

"Pretty enough. Care for any other details, or can I cut to the chase?"

"By all means." She didn't want to hear about strolls through the romantic city built on islands, or how they'd toasted each other in sidewalk cafés and enjoyed the Royal Ballet.

She and Tom had done all those things during the two years they'd lived in the Swedish capital. Marnie had been pleasantly surprised that the cool summers were followed by mild winters, thanks to southwesterly winds from the Atlantic Ocean.

She remembered one weekend when they'd sailed to a small island in the archipelago that lay between Sweden and Finland, and stayed at an old cabin that might have been built by Vikings. Well, it wasn't quite that old, but it was rustic.

They'd been deliciously alone, with nothing to concentrate on but each other. If he'd taken Elise to one of those islands, she didn't want to hear about it.

"A few weeks after I met her, I was reassigned to Rome." Tom leaned against the refrigerator, his expression unreadable.

"Did you invite her to come with you?" Marnie cringed as soon as the words were out. She knew she was setting herself up for more needle jabs of discomfort.

"No," Tom said.

"Why not?"

He coughed. "You think I should have?"

"If you loved her."

"I didn't. She didn't love me, either." He shrugged. "As far as I knew, we'd had a good time and were ready to move on. And please don't give me the Uncle Norbert lecture."

"I don't intend to. So she was pregnant when you moved?" From her grandmother's room, Marnie could hear the computer game chirping and clanging. But the only thing she could focus on was the way Tom's face filled with regret.

"She must have been. I had no idea," he said. "I sent her my new address, but she didn't write. I'd have gone back. I'd have supported her, even married her, I guess, although I suspect we'd have made each other miserable."

The way we did? Marnie wondered, but refused to say it. Besides, until near the end, their marriage had been the happiest time of her life.

"As you know, the reassignment was a promotion, and that meant more work," Tom said. "They keep me busy."

The work of an embassy, Marnie knew, involved such everyday tasks as issuing visas, assisting Americans abroad and monitoring local political and economic conditions. More seriously, the staff supported the ambassador and other state department officials in setting up conferences and negotiations.

"You didn't go back to visit Elise once you'd moved?" she asked.

"No. She never suggested it, and neither did I." Outside, darkness had descended. In the kitchen, fluorescent lights banished the gloom, except inside Marnie. "I'm ashamed to say I rarely thought of her."

Why had he jumped into the bed of a woman who meant so little to him? Yet Tom hadn't behaved much differently from a thousand other men, Marnie supposed. And he'd had a right to date other women, once he was no longer married.

"Last year," he continued, "I got a letter from an attorney in Stockholm. He said Elise had died suddenly of an aneurysm. My name was listed on her son's birth certificate, so he contacted me to take custody."

"You must have been stunned!"

He thumped the refrigerator for emphasis. "Heck, yes. At first, I guess I was in denial, because I was determined not to let anything tie me down. I figured Elise's parents would want Cody, but they didn't. Their health isn't good."

Marnie's heart went out to the little boy, left alone and unwanted. "How old was he?"

"Eighteen months," Tom said. "At the time, I had no clue what that meant in terms of his development. I had no clue what anything meant."

"But you took him in."

"I hired Olivia and figured, okay, I'll do my duty,

give my son a home and an education," he said. "That's more than I got from my parents."

It was obvious that, at some point, he'd fallen in love with the child. "What changed your mind?"

"He grew on me." Tom gave her a lopsided grin. "Maybe I needed him to fill the void that—" He paused. "To fill a void I didn't know I had. Or maybe it's his personality that makes him so lovable. Who knows? He's mine now."

Marnie's heart swelled with yearning and a certain satisfaction. She'd always known Tom would make a wonderful dad, despite his father's poor example.

Like so many survivors of difficult childhoods, Tom had grown strong. He'd used his skill at overcoming hardship to make a better life for himself— and, through his work, a better world for others.

Marnie knew what she had to ask next, but it frightened her. More than that, it terrified her, because it revealed her own vulnerability.

She had to phrase it so it would sound casual, so Tom wouldn't see the raw wound that refused to heal. She didn't want his pity; she just wanted an answer.

"So now that you're crazy about Cody," she said, "you probably want a whole houseful of kids. With the right woman, of course."

Her words hung in the air. Fragile as etched-glass wind chimes, they echoed through Marnie's bones.

"More kids?" Tom regarded her as if she'd lost her mind. "What on earth for?"

"I figured—"

He interrupted impatiently. "Marnie, Cody and I are a couple of orphans clinging to each other in a storm. It's a fluke that we hit it off so well. I'm still the same man I always was, so don't kid yourself.''

Springing from her chair, she went to put the food on the table. She didn't want Tom to see the tears that threatened to wreck her self-control.

Why had she been so stupid as to hope he might have changed? He didn't want to have a family with her now, any more than he had four years ago.

''Thanks for telling me about Elise.'' She carried the glass baking dish across the kitchen. ''Would you call Granny and Cody to dinner?''

''Marnie.'' Tom stood motionless, his arms at his sides. ''I wish…''

''What?'' Frowning at the browned cheese, she set the hot pan on a trivet.

''I wish you'd stop shutting me out! At least look at me!''

She bit back the angry words that sprang to mind: *You think I'm shutting you out? What about what you're doing to me?* They didn't need another fruit-less argument. ''I'm doing the best I can.''

Tom released an impatient breath. ''I suppose we both are,'' he said, and strode from the room.

Marnie was grateful when she heard her grand-mother's footsteps tapping briskly down the hall. Now they would have to keep the conversation general.

Jolene claimed the head of the table and sank into her chair. ''After dinner,'' she announced, ''I will read to Cody.''

Behind her, Tom escorted his son into the kitchen. Cody, his hands pink from washing, scampered to the table.

"I'm sure he'll enjoy that," Tom said.

"And you two," Jolene continued, "will go into the attic and bring down the Christmas decorations. Watch out for the racoon or the owl. I've heard something nesting up there."

"I can handle the decorations," Marnie said quickly. "Tom will want to put his son to bed."

"He'll go with you." Jolene helped herself to a slice of bread and set a piece on Cody's plate. "We need a man around here, and while we've got one, let's take advantage of him."

"Okay, he can go," Marnie said. "I'll clean the kitchen."

Jolene fixed her granddaughter with a frown. "Cody and I will take care of the dishes. You will bring down the tree ornaments tonight. I have my reasons."

"Which are…?"

"While you're in this house, young lady, you will follow orders! No cross-examinations, no quibbling, no lollygagging. The same goes for you, Tom Jakes!"

Marnie glanced at her ex-husband, dismayed at how obviously they were being manipulated into going upstairs together. But he merely saluted her grandmother and said, "Yes, ma'am!"

"Well?" The older woman regarded Marnie with mock sternness. "Is he the only one around here with any respect for old age?"

She lifted her chin. "Whatever you say, Jolene."

It annoyed her that Tom didn't object to her grandmother's shenanigans. In fact, judging by his smug

smile, he didn't at all mind putting Marnie in an awkward position.

If he wanted a battle of wills this weekend, he
would get one, she decided.

And he would lose.

Chapter Four

"This is crazy, coming up here at night," Marnie groused as they reached the top of the attic stairs. "Who can see anything?"

"I can see fine," murmured Tom. He was, she realized, bound and determined to provoke her.

"Sure, if you squint," she snapped. "Then maybe you can see your hand in front of your face. Just barely."

During the day, plenty of light shone through the front and back windows. Now, however, the illumination from one old floor lamp threw the large room into a confusing welter of shadows and glare.

"There's got to be another switch." Marnie searched around on the wall, without luck. Finally Tom managed to turn on the overhead chandelier, an incongruously modern contraption made of etched-glass panels that resembled wind chimes.

The fixture, which Granny's neighbor had installed at her request, provided clearer illumination, but only in the center of the room. Marnie stared about her, wondering where the decorations could be stashed.

The sloping roof reached nearly to the floor on both

sides of the attic. She shuddered at the thought that something might indeed be nesting under there. The only noncreepy possibility was Granny's cat, Miss Lacy, but she preferred the barn to the house.

"Cold?" Tom's voice, close to her shoulder, startled her.

"What?"

"You're shivering."

"It's fear," she said.

"Of me?" He looked at her sharply.

"Of things that go bump in the night. Let's just find the ornaments and get out of here, all right?"

"Suits me."

To her left lay an open area of wooden flooring where, years ago, she and her grandparents used to stage rainy-day picnics. Along the edge, beneath the sloped ceiling, were stored suitcases, several boxes marked Clothes, and an old mirror.

To her right, across a broad aisle, old chairs and tables crowded together. When she came closer, Marnie spotted a trunk with a shiny lock. She pried at it, but couldn't get it open. "What do you suppose this is?"

Tom knelt to take his turn at the hasp. "Someone's been here recently. It's hardly even dusty. You're sure this isn't something you shipped back from Stockholm?"

"I didn't have a trunk this color," Marnie said. "In any case, I don't see why Granny would have bothered locking up the Christmas stuff."

Restlessly, she circled behind the staircase, where built-in cabinets lined the wall, and ran smack into a sticky cobweb. With a shudder, she wiped it off. "Spiders!"

"You're not going to let a little thing like that scare you off, are you?" Tom walked past Marnie, waving his arms to clear the passageway. "There doesn't seem to be any more. You must have hit the only one."

"Just my luck." Marching past him, she circled into the open picnic area. He was right—she didn't run into any more webs. "Mrs. Wheedles must vacuum up here."

Mrs. Wheedles was a roly-poly lady from town who cleaned houses with ruthless efficiency. Marnie paid her to come to Granny's place once a week.

"Didn't she have a daughter in our class?" Tom asked as he produced a flashlight from his pocket and examined the cabinets.

"Sure, Bethany Wheedles. She looks like a younger version of her mom. It's remarkable how many kids turn into their parents when they grow up."

His back stiffened. "I suppose a lot of people believe that."

"I didn't mean *you!*"

Tom was nothing like his father. Unemployed and mean tempered, Furnell Jakes had drunk himself to death in his cabin outside town.

After he died, Tom and Marnie had driven back from college to attend the small burial service. They'd been the only mourners.

"I know you didn't mean it that way," he conceded raggedly. "But other people... You never really saw what they were like. How they treated me."

In the diffused light, his face took on a tightness that reminded her of the way he'd looked in high school. Angry and always on guard. Except with her.

Marnie stopped flipping through boxes. ''Tell me,'' she said. ''Tell me what they were like.''

His flashlight beam paused on some interior shelves. ''Remember how surprised everyone was at our senior awards ceremony, when I won an honor certificate in history?''

''Everyone except the teachers,'' Marnie pointed out. ''But no one claimed you didn't deserve it.''

''Not right then. And certainly not in front of you.'' He smacked the doors shut and moved to the next cabinet.

''Who said something? When?''

''Remember graduation?''

''Well, of course!'' Marnie supposed she ought to resume searching for the decorations, but she wanted to concentrate on Tom's words. ''Are you telling me something happened that I didn't know about? I thought you enjoyed yourself.''

That day had passed in a happy blur, but now that she thought about it, Tom had retreated into his shell after the ceremony. She'd attributed the change to his shyness at being around so many people.

''Graduation *was* special.'' He poked through a box, and she heard metal parts rattling. ''Dad stayed away, thank goodness, and your grandmother cheered as loudly for me as she did for you.''

Marnie smiled at the memory of Jolene hooting and whooping. ''She was a real trooper.''

Tom's expression sobered. ''Then you went off to

have your picture taken with your girlfriends. Betty and— What was her name?''

"Luanne." They'd lost touch after Luanne moved away from Ryder's Crossing a few years later, but Betty was still a close pal.

"While you were gone, Luke Skerritt and Robby Jones came over.'' Luke had been class president, while his friend Robby edited the school paper.

Marnie got an uneasy feeling. Luke and Robby had grown up to be men she liked and respected, but back in high school they'd been puffed up with their own importance. "What did they say?''

"They wanted to congratulate me on pulling it off. They were being sarcastic, of course.'' Tom lifted down a toolbox, checked the contents and put it back. "They implied that you'd done my papers for me.''

"That's ridiculous!'' Marnie had heard some speculation along those lines from her girlfriends but had laughed it off. "I'm not half as good a writer as you are!''

"You corrected my spelling and grammar,'' Tom pointed out.

"Yes, but you had such fascinating ideas, and you did the research!'' She'd been in awe of the concepts that tumbled from Tom's brain, once he'd brought his intelligence to bear on his schoolwork. "You earned that award, one hundred percent!''

He closed the cabinet. "Robby advised me to make my career somewhere other than Ryder's Crossing. He let me know he considered me a fraud and that someday he would take over his father's newspaper and expose me, if I had the nerve to stick around.''

"He must have been jealous!" But Marnie knew that wasn't the whole truth.

Tom had been too closemouthed to speak up in class, so the other kids hadn't seen the workings of his mind firsthand. They'd never understood his transformation from near flunk-out to brilliant student.

Although she couldn't excuse Luke's and Robby's meanness on graduation day, they'd no doubt believed they were right. As teenagers, both boys had had a strong sense of justice and no mercy for anyone who cheated.

"I don't suppose it helped that you and I went to college together," Tom said. "They probably think you did my papers for me there, too."

"They certainly know I didn't take your Foreign Service exam!" Marnie pointed out. "I didn't go through the institute with you, either."

Applicants to the Foreign Service underwent extensive testing and evaluation. They had to demonstrate everything from strong communication skills to an ability to work with others. They also studied languages and the customs of other nations at the Foreign Service Institute in Washington, D.C.

Appointments and promotions were competitive. Tom had succeeded on his own merit.

"Who knows?" He shrugged. "In their minds, I'll always be Furnell Jakes's son. But that was good advice they gave me about making my career outside Ryder's Crossing. They can keep their precious town—I'll take the rest of the world."

Marnie itched to remind him that, small and insignificant as it might be, Ryder's Crossing was *her* world. But what would be the point? How ironic, that she'd helped the man she loved outgrow this place, and in the process he'd outgrown her, as well.

If only she didn't still ache to touch him, to press her cheek against his chest and feel his arms around her. To kiss away the tight expression on his face and make him come alive against her and inside her.

In her heart they were still husband and wife. But not in his heart.

Tom's words merely confirmed what she already knew, that it was time she truly let him go. Marnie supposed that ought to be her goal this weekend, for both their sakes: to make peace and move on. It was the only way she would ever be able to find another man to love, and to have children of her own.

Still, she didn't want to leave him with the wrong impression about the people they'd known. In fact, she had an obligation to explain just how much things had changed. "High school was fourteen years ago," she pointed out. "You'd hardly recognize those fellows now."

"Oh?" His mouth quirked. "Tell me Luke's taken holy orders and Robby writes nothing but love songs. Surprise me."

"Well, not quite but..."

He came closer, his muscular frame dominating Marnie's field of vision. They ought to be having this conversation lying in each other's arms after making love, she thought wistfully. Or at least sitting curled together on the old couch in the corner.

"So what are my old buddies doing?" he asked, with ironic emphasis on the word *buddies*.

"Pretty much what you would expect." She sighed. "Robby's managing editor of the local paper, now that his dad's retired. And Luke's senior vice president of Skerritt Construction. They built the new mall you passed on your way into town.''

''Senior vice president?'' Tom clicked his tongue, pretending to be impressed. ''That's quite an achievement at the age of thirty-two. Of course, it's not quite so hard when you're the owner's son.''

''You think he doesn't realize that?'' Marnie could see that her defense of their former schoolmates was making her ex-husband bristle, but she had to be fair. ''Look, all I'm saying is that you and I aren't the only ones who've matured.''

''You actually like those guys now?'' His edgy tone put her on guard.

''They're not my best friends, but I respect them,'' she said. ''Luke and Robby organized the new chamber of commerce, which this town needs, and I'm on the board.''

''Congratulations.'' To her surprise, Tom sounded genuinely pleased. ''Marnie, you deserve the honor. I don't mean to be a poor sport. The truth is, I admire the way you've built your business and taken care of Granny at the same time.''

''Jolene?'' She chuckled. ''Nobody takes care of her! She's as independent as ever.''

''And as determined to run everybody else's life.'' Fondness replaced his former sarcasm. ''The annoying thing is that she does a better job of it than we like to admit.''

''I'm still not ready to admit it,'' she said.

''Well, she's got a whole four days to work on us.'' After tucking the flashlight into his pocket, he rubbed his hands lightly up Marnie's arms. Tremors of desire fanned down her body.

"Tired of fighting?" she asked. "I know I am."

"Were we fighting?"

"Poking at scabs, anyway." She ought to back away, but she couldn't. There was a topic she'd promised to broach, and somehow she had to work around to it.

"You don't have unhappy memories, do you?" In the silent attic, Tom's voice sounded louder than usual.

Marnie's only bad memories were of those last months in Stockholm, when he seemed to resent everything she said, and she hurt so much she could barely look at him. Now all she wanted to do was memorize every inch of his face.

She was saved the need to answer when his arms closed around her. As his lips met hers, her emotional armor melted, and so did thoughts of anything but him.

Past and present lost all meaning. There was only the reality of desire engulfing them. Marnie clung to Tom's firm shoulders, to his hard mouth.

His tongue sketched the inner curve of her lip. Beneath her hands, through his shirt, his skin glowed white-hot.

A rustling noise seemed at first to come from their own subtly rhythmic movements, and then Marnie heard a scraping from a corner of the attic. She felt a strong urge to ignore it, but Tom must have heard it, too. He pulled away from their embrace with an oath and thrust himself protectively in front of her.

"Who's there?" he demanded.

The only answer was a scritch-scratching like claws on bare floor. Tom snatched the flashlight and played it beneath the eaves.

Marnie had to clear her throat before she could speak. "That wasn't an owl."

"A raccoon, maybe, or a squirrel." Crouching, he peered into the inky depths. "It's gone, whatever it was." Then came a dry bark of disbelief.

"What?"

"Whatever it was knocked over this box—there's a colored bulb poking out. Talk about luck!"

Marnie joined him in the corner. Sure enough, a strand of Christmas tree lights jutted from a gap in the cardboard. "There's another box behind it."

He lifted the lid. "Silver tinsel, and glass ornaments underneath. Looks like we've found our treasure."

They had a perfect excuse to leave the attic, and Marnie knew they ought to. Reluctantly she picked up one of the boxes. It was light, and she hoisted it easily.

"Wait a minute. We're not through talking," Tom said.

"You call that talking?"

He grasped the other side of the box. "Are you going to run downstairs the way you ran home from Sweden? Isn't it time we hashed things out?"

"Tom, everything's settled."

"No, it isn't!" They faced each other across the cardboard box, each stubbornly maintaining a grip. "It doesn't matter how far apart we live or how long we've been separated. You belong to me. Can't you feel it?"

Of course she did, but this was crazy. Their chemistry might be as strong as ever, but it solved nothing. Worse, it would only bring more grief.

"We should go downstairs."

"That's it? That's all you can say?" he demanded.

"What do you want from me?" The cry tore from her. "I know it isn't just chemistry, but Tom, what else can we have?"

A muscle twitched in his jaw. "Sorry. When you said people change, I thought maybe you were including yourself."

He released the box, seized the other one and started down the stairs. Marnie stood frozen.

He'd told her bluntly that he didn't want more kids and that he had no intention of remaining in their hometown. What did he expect from her? To give up all her dreams, just because he snapped his fingers and asked her to come back?

She nearly called after him, but she couldn't find the words. Maybe, she reflected unhappily, it was because she had no idea what to say.

Clutching the box as if it were a life preserver, she followed after him.

TOM HAD ALMOST REACHED the ground floor when the doorbell rang. Great, he thought irritably. The last thing he was in the mood for was to be sociable with guests.

No one could turn his emotions upside down and inside out like Marnie. He'd sworn to himself before he made this trip that he wouldn't let her get to him, that they could just be friends. Well, that resolve hadn't lasted long, had it?

Not that he blamed her. And he hadn't exactly told the truth, either. He'd said that she belonged to him, when the opposite was true. He'd belonged to her from that first day in high school.

They were meant to be together. Their bodies fit, and so did their minds. The intellectual curiosity they shared gave them the capacity to stimulate each other in ways that went far beyond sex.

Why couldn't she see that it was useless fighting it? She needed to accept him the way he was, with his dark recesses as well as his enthusiasms. Without unconditional love, what hope could they have?

He loved her to the very foundation of his soul. It drove him wild to be held at bay.

Thank goodness for his years of diplomatic training and experience. Without them, Tom didn't know how he could have pasted on a civilized expression as Jolene opened the front door to admit a noisy group of strangers bearing a Christmas tree, which they'd apparently cut at her request.

Amid a few snowflakes blowing in on a blast of cold air, there was much hugging and exchanging of season's greetings. These expanded to include Marnie, who edged by Tom to welcome the newcomers, and then Jolene made introductions.

The cheerful fortyish couple were Lew and Helen Ryan, who had bought a neighboring farm a few years ago and now rented Jolene's fields. They were the parents of the three freckle-faced kids grinning at Cody.

There was one more person, a man about Tom's age, with mild gray eyes and the solid build of a farmer. ''Helen's younger brother,'' Jolene said by way of introduction, "Guthrie Phillips, who recently moved here from Chattanooga."

Under other circumstances, Tom might have liked Guthrie. But the man's gaze had a way of drifting past everyone to fix on Marnie.

She was hanging coats on a rack and asking if anyone wanted coffee, which they declined. Tom wondered whether her face had become flushed from the chill air or whether she'd noticed Guthrie's attention.

He'd never been the jealous type, and he didn't intend to start now. Assuming his best diplomatic mien, Tom shook hands with Lew and his brother-in-law.

"You kids go play on the computer," Jolene directed. The children, supervised by their mother, gleefully trailed Cody to the bedroom. "Gentlemen, I'll show you where I want the tree. Marnie, I don't suppose you found the stand to put it in, did you?"

"It might be in this box." She knelt and rummaged through the contents.

"Why don't I help with that?" Guthrie hurried to her side. "Miss Afton, you'll get all dirty."

"Oh, it's too late to prevent that! We've been up in the attic." As if to illustrate the point, a lock of light brown hair strayed across Marnie's cheek. She swept it back with an impatient hand.

Tom wished Guthrie wouldn't ogle every move she made. Okay, maybe he himself watched Marnie like a hawk, but that was different. He was, in the loosest sense of the word, family.

"Mr. Jakes, would you mind helping me with this tree?" Lew Ryan asked. "Maybe you'd like to put on some work gloves first. These needles are sharp."

Tom might work in an office, but he was no light-weight. "Thanks, but I can handle it." He hefted one end of the tree and tried to ignore the sting of the needles. What was a little pain compared to a man's dignity?

From the box Marnie produced a white enamel-plated metal bowl with three braced feet. A center support had a hole for the tree trunk. "Here it is!"

"I'll take it to the parlor," Guthrie offered. "Or would you rather I fetched some water for the tree?"

"You take it. I'll get the watering pot." When she stood up, Marnie arched her back to unkink it. The position highlighted the tantalizing shape of her body beneath the peasant blouse, and the visitor didn't miss one inch of the view.

The man was incredibly presumptuous. Tom couldn't imagine how other people could stand him.

It was only as he and Lew steered the ten-foot pine into the living room that Tom caught sight of the smirk on Jolene's face. Why, the old lady had set up this situation to make him jealous! he reflected with grudging admiration.

It was a cheap trick. Yet she hadn't manufactured Guthrie Phillips's interest in Marnie. The newcomer just hadn't had time to figure out that she didn't return it.

Or did she?

Guthrie lived on the Ryans' farm, right here near Ryder's Crossing, while Tom's home was several thousand miles away. This Christmas, the man might not get to spend much time with Marnie—in fact, he'd spend not a single minute alone with her, if Tom had anything to do with it—but he would have days and weeks and months afterward.

Grumpily Tom reflected that Guthrie probably wanted kids, lots of wholesome freckled ones like his niece and nephews. Well, okay, so Guthrie didn't have any freckles himself, but he was too darned wholesome for Tom's taste. Boring. Ordinary. Unworthy of so special a woman.

"Tom!" Jolene called from the rocking chair where she'd settled. "If you would stop tilting that tree like you wanted to stab someone with it, maybe Lew could get it screwed in straight!"

"Sorry." Frowning, he shoved the tree upright, sending a shower of needles over Guthrie, who had knelt to help his brother-in-law. The man merely brushed off the needles and regarded Tom quizzically.

It was time to establish friendly communications before he embarrassed himself. "So you're new to Ryder's Crossing?"

Guthrie nodded. "Helen and I grew up near Chattanooga. We're farm folks. I tried working in a store for a while, but city life don't suit me."

The man's grammar might not be perfect, but Tom didn't want to become a snob like the boys who'd belittled him in high school. "So, you planning to stay in the area?"

"Oh, yes, indeed," said Guthrie. "I'd like to buy a farm of my own."

"Not too much land available around here, I shouldn't think." Tom had noted several new housing developments as well as a mall outside town. "The builders must be acquiring most of the land."

"I reckon I can find something not too far off, if

I'm patient," Guthrie said. "When there's something I want, I know how to bide my time till I get it."

The statement carried a double meaning, one that rankled a little. Where Marnie was concerned Guthrie definitely had time on his side.

"Guth may not look it, but he's tenacious as a bulldog," Lew confirmed as he fixed the tree into place. "Mrs. Afton, does that look straight to you?"

Jolene assessed the tree's angle. "Sure does."

After Lew finished tightening the screws, the two neighbors went into the hall to retrieve the boxes. Seizing the moment, Jolene said, "Guthrie's a nice fellow, don't you think?"

"Give it a rest, Granny," Tom grumbled.

"Eh?" She frowned as if she hadn't heard.

"I got the point." He met her gaze. "You want to make me jealous."

She winked. "And it's working, too."

Tom wanted to deny it, but couldn't. Instead, he said, "Marnie has better sense than to marry the first man who comes along."

"You can't expect her to wait forever for you to come to your senses."

She'd never made such a bald statement to him before, although Tom had certainly picked up hints in her letters and in their occasional phone conversations. "Is that what you expect? That something's going to happen between us this weekend?"

"My attic may be a little dusty, but it doesn't make two people get that disheveled all by itself," she replied tartly.

Tom could feel his face turning scarlet. No one had

ever been able to read him as well as Granny Afton, not even Marnie.

Before he could say anything in his own defense, Marnie lugged in a large watering pot. Guthrie trailed her with one of the ornament boxes, and Lew followed with the other one.

"Is it okay for me to fill it now?" she asked.

"Fill away," said Granny.

Once Marnie finished watering, Tom knelt to spread the tree skirt over the stand. Smoothing the wrinkles from the fabric reminded him of the many special details he'd almost forgotten about Christmas.

How wonderful a fresh pine tree smelled, for instance. How the colored glass ornaments gleamed with hidden depths as they were hung on the branches. How ordinary tinsel could appear touched with magic.

Tom was amazed to discover his bad temper dissipating. He felt a glow of good fellowship that extended even toward Guthrie Phillips.

He couldn't blame the man for flirting with Marnie. As she stood on a chair to fix a hand-carved angel atop the tree, the lamplight turned her brown hair into a halo and made her eyes sparkle.

Guthrie had probably never met anyone quite like her. Tom certainly hadn't. In all the world, there was only one Marnie Afton.

He had to find a way to win her back.

Chapter Five

Marnie didn't see how she could fall asleep, knowing Tom lay in a bed on the same floor, although in the opposite corner of the house.

It could have been worse, she told herself as she tossed beneath the heirloom quilt. Granny had originally instructed Tom and his son to sleep in the den directly across the second-floor hallway from Marnie's room.

Instead, he'd chosen the smaller guest room at the back of the house, saying Norbert and Linda could have the bigger chamber, when they came. But Marnie suspected that Tom, too, preferred to put some distance between them.

Certainly it would be awkward to lie here listening to the pull-out couch creak whenever he turned over. Picturing him lying there, his blond hair rumpled on the pillow, his broad shoulders making a mountain of the covers....

Darn it, she needed to go to sleep! Why wouldn't her mind turn off?

Staring into the inky darkness, Marnie realized that, even in a small town like Ryder's Crossing, she'd grown accustomed to a certain level of traffic noise at night. Not to mention the lights shining from neighboring houses.

Tonight clouds blocked the moon, and except for the occasional rustle of a tree branch outside, she heard nothing. The light snowfall must have driven even night birds and stray dogs to take shelter.

The darkness and silence disturbed rather than soothed her. Every nerve felt ruffled.

She could still feel Tom's mouth on hers, from when they'd embraced in the attic. His barely leashed hunger had released her own.

No wonder she'd once mistaken his friendship for true love. They fit together so naturally and sparked such a burning need, it was hard to imagine he could feel that way with anyone else. Yet obviously he had with Elise.

What Marnie didn't understand was why he was behaving this way now, kissing her senseless and glaring at Guthrie like a jealous guard dog. She knew Tom too well to believe he was merely playing a game.

Most likely he didn't understand his own reasons. Maybe he was lonely, despite his busy schedule and his son. He'd said himself that one reason he bonded so strongly with Cody was because the boy filled a gap in his life.

As for the way Tom had acted toward Guthrie, men were by nature territorial. Anyone in the diplomatic field knew that people sometimes fought to the death over land they had no real use for.

Rolling over, Marnie closed her eyes and tried again to doze. Defiantly her mind kept racing.

She'd mentioned the chamber of commerce to Tom, but his dislike of Luke and Robby had prevented her from saying more. Still, the chamber board had given Marnie a mission to accomplish, and she was going to have to bring it up sooner or later.

It was unlikely Tom would agree. He would never move back to Ryder's Crossing.

What she ought to do was fall in love with someone kind and steady, like Guthrie, and forget all about Tom Jakes. If only she could figure out how.

In the middle of trying to talk herself into the impossible, Marnie must have fallen asleep. She had no awareness of time passing until she heard a knock on her door, or perhaps it was part of a dream. On coming awake, however, she was puzzled to hear a scuffing noise coming from the stairs.

Could someone be climbing to the attic? Sleep-dazed, she peered at the bedside clock.

The glow-in-the-dark numerals had faded over the years, but apparently the clouds had cleared outside, because the moon shone brightly enough for her to see that it was nearly 3:00 a.m. Who would be prowling around at this hour?

Granny sometimes awoke in the wee hours and suffered from insomnia, but her solution was to read the Bible. Besides, in her condition, she certainly wasn't going to go sneaking up the steps.

Neither was Tom, or, at least, Marnie couldn't imagine why he would. That only left one person: Cody. A little child in a strange place might well go wandering.

She threw back the quilt, admitting a rush of chill

air. Quickly she stuck her feet into slippers and pulled a velour robe over her nightgown.

Cody might be sleepwalking, or perhaps he'd gone in search of the bathroom. He would have had to pass the stairs to get there.

Marnie took a flashlight from her bedside drawer, and found to her disgust that the batteries were dead. Telling herself that at this point her eyes had adjusted to the dark, anyway, she hurried into the hall and heard a scrabbling sound overhead.

Someone, or some animal, was definitely in the attic. She hoped Cody wasn't going to find himself face-to-face with a raccoon, which could be dangerous if cornered.

Anxiously she pattered up the stairs. At the top, moonglow bathed the space in a yellow light, creating an eerie landscape of shapes and shadows.

Surely a child would be too frightened to venture into this place alone. On the other hand, weren't two-year-olds supposed to be fearless?

A flurry of scritch-scratching from one side made Marnie's heart skip a beat. "Cody?" she called.

"*Ciao*, Marnie!" chirped a little voice.

Smiling at his gleeful tone, she reached for the switch to turn on the overhead light. It wasn't where she thought it would be, and she remembered that she'd had trouble locating it earlier. "Are you all right?" she asked as she fumbled with what appeared to be a floor lamp.

"Come here! Hurry!" piped the boy's voice.

The moonlight showed her a small, dark shape about a dozen feet away. He was gazing toward a jumble of suitcases and other items stored beneath the rafters.

Marnie discovered that she was trying to switch on a hat rack, and gave up the attempt. "Be careful! Raccoons can be dangerous."

"No, look!" Cody said. "It's an angel!"

He must have spotted some Christmas decoration that they'd dropped, she mused as she approached. When she crouched to his level, however, Marnie realized that he was gazing into a mirror.

A stray moonbeam must be filtering through the overhead glass fixture, because a faint rainbow appeared in the glass. "Oh, honey, that's not an angel. Do you know what a prism is?"

He shook his head without taking his gaze from the image.

"It's like a rainbow," she said.

"Un arcobaleno?" He clapped his hands in excitement. "The angel made it!"

Nothing she said seemed to dissuade him from his fantasy, Marnie reflected ruefully. "That's a lovely idea, but the only angel around here is the one on the Christmas tree." *And this little sweetheart,* she thought, gathering him into her arms.

Cody snuggled against her, but he wasn't giving up. "I saw her in my room."

"The angel?"

He nodded, his baby breath tickling her cheek. "I followed her."

"What did she look like?"

"She had wings and a pink dress. Also a..." He searched for the word he wanted, then pantomimed a circle above his head.

"A halo?" Marnie tried to figure out a rational explanation. The boy could have been dreaming about the angel on the tree. He might have awakened and seen something moving in the hall, but she couldn't imagine what, unless Miss Lacy had sneaked into the house to escape the cold. "Maybe the cat," she said.

"Cat?" Cody asked with interest.

"Miss Lacy." Holding the child soothed Marnie; she could have sworn her brain waves were shifting into a more relaxed pattern. "You can meet her tomorrow."

"She hit your door," Cody said.

"Hit my door?" Marnie repeated.

"Bam-bam." He tapped one fist against an open palm. "Then up she went."

Marnie *had* heard a knock, she recalled in surprise. Although Granny bragged that Miss Lacy was smart, even she wouldn't claim the cat went around knocking on doors. "Are you sure you didn't do that yourself?"

"It was the angel." The boy yawned.

Marnie persisted, hoping to piece together the whole story. "So you followed the angel up here?"

"She called my name," Cody said. "Then *pfft!* Gone. And here is a...rainbow."

Marnie glanced around, but nothing stirred in the attic. No one had gone down the stairs, yet they appeared to be alone. "Let's go find your daddy. No more coming up here, Cody. You could get hurt."

"Angels don't hurt," he said, but obediently took her hand.

On the second floor they nearly ran into Tom. With his hair askew and his robe loosely fastened, he had obviously just awakened and gone in search of his son.

"He was in the attic," Marnie said without preface. "He claims he saw an angel and followed her upstairs."

Tom swept the boy into his arms. "Daddy was worried, Cody."

"I'm okay." The little boy wiggled happily. "Come up and see the rainbow."

Marnie told him about the prism and the unexplained knocking. "I'm sure my son did that," Tom said. "He's an active little tyke. Come on, Cody, I'll read you a story till you fall asleep."

"And no more wandering!" Marnie couldn't resist adding.

"That' s right." Over Cody's head, Tom shot her a grateful look. "I'm glad you found him. I was about to search downstairs. I thought maybe he'd gone to look at the Christmas tree."

For a second Marnie allowed herself a fantasy: that she and Tom were still married, and this was their child, and they were sharing a moment that would become an amusing family memory.

Remember the angel in the attic? they would say. *Cody claimed it knocked on Mommy's door!*

Only she wasn't Mommy. And she would never share such moments with Tom, because they weren't going to have a future together.

Marnie pulled her robe tighter, but this time the chill came from inside. "Good night," she said in a muffled tone, and escaped to her room.

SHE AWOKE to the smell of cinnamon muffins baking downstairs. The warm covers tempted Marnie to burrow in, but her stomach insisted on having its way.

To her amazement she'd fallen asleep quickly after last night's adventure. Tom and Cody must have arisen early, judging by the activity below.

How much snow had fallen? Marnie wondered. At the window she peered out to note only a light dusting. It sparkled in the sunshine and was probably already on the way to melting.

She hoped the weather was equally good in Chicago, or that at least Mike would get his car fixed. With luck someone would arrive by tonight to provide a welcome buffer between her and Tom.

She slipped into the bathroom and showered, then dressed in jeans and a red pullover with a band of green reindeer knitted across the chest.

On the landing Marnie glanced down the far hallway toward the guest room and was surprised to see the door shut. If those two were still abed, who was cooking?

She went down the stairs to the sound of laughter from below. It was her grandmother and a man, she thought in surprise, and they sounded awfully cozy.

Curious, Marnie hurried to the kitchen. She saw Dr. Spindler standing at the sink, scrubbing a muffin tin. Although she'd known the doctor all her life, she was surprised to see him performing such a domestic chore.

"Good morning!" he announced. At eighty-two, Artie Spindler stood ramrod straight, and his shock of white hair showed no signs of thinning. Instead of his usual baggy jacket, the doctor wore a handsome V-neck sweater over a button-down shirt.

Town legend had it that right out of medical school he'd enlisted to fight in World War II and that he'd parachuted in with the D-Day invasion to treat injured soldiers. His no-nonsense manner had always reminded Marnie of the military, but it was countered by twinkling eyes and a ready hand with lollipops for children after vaccinations.

"Merry Christmas," she said, although the holiday wasn't until the day after tomorrow. "Did you come to check on my grandmother?"

"Yes, and look what she roped me into doing." He indicated a plate of cinnamon muffins on the counter.

Marnie spotted Jolene resting on a chair at the table. She wore a bland expression but her cheeks were pink, as if from excitement.

"You fixed all this yourself?" Marnie asked the doctor. "I never thought Granny would let a man take over her kitchen."

"I gave directions," said her grandmother.

"As if I needed them!" Artie harrumphed. "I've been a widower for ten years. If I hadn't learned to cook by now, I'd be a pretty sorry individual."

Dr. Spindler, who was semiretired, lived about a mile away, and Marnie knew he sometimes dropped in to play Scrabble with Granny. She'd assumed it was a way of keeping tabs on a longtime patient, but it was obvious the two had become good friends.

"It's kind of you to help out," she said. "I know Granny shouldn't exert herself too much, in her condition."

Artie coughed and turned to dry the muffin pan.

"Do you have a cold?"

"Something stuck in my throat," said the doctor. "By the way, there's coffee made."

"Thanks." With a twinge of guilt, Marnie noticed that it was nearly nine o'clock. Not only had she slept later than usual, but she felt as if she should be heading to town to open the store.

She supposed she could drive in and check on Betty, but she knew her old friend wanted to prove she could handle the job on her own. After twelve years as a homemaker, Betty loved the challenge and took pride in her work.

If any problems occurred, she would call, Marnie reminded herself, and went to get some coffee. Standing at the window as she stirred in sugar and milk, she noticed a couple of deer browsing far off in one of the fields.

"Did you hear the noise upstairs last night?" she asked her grandmother as she took a muffin and sat at the table. Artie joined them. "About 3:00 a.m.?"

"Noise?" Jolene finished eating her muffin before stating, "I can't say that I did."

That wasn't surprising. Her room lay directly below Marnie's, far removed from the goings-on.

She explained about Cody's wandering. "I hope he isn't going up there again tonight."

"Sleep disturbances aren't unusual at his age," the doctor noted. "But as he adjusts to his surroundings, the problem should diminish."

"He's only got three days," Marnie pointed out. "They're flying back to Rome on Sunday, right?"

"Right." Jolene frowned at Artie. "Why are you tearing that muffin into little pieces? Just butter it and eat it!"

"Tastes better this way," muttered the doctor.

A loud thumping interrupted them, and Cody galloped into the room. "Cody hungry!" He snatched a muffin from the counter.

"Cody!" Tom followed his son from the hall. The dark indigo of his Italian pullover gave his azure eyes a startling intensity.

Artie stood and shook Tom's hand before either of the women could speak. Tom wore a puzzled expression at finding the doctor in the kitchen, but was tactful enough not to say anything.

"I'll get the boy some milk," Artie said. "You help yourself to our bakeoff special."

"Thanks," Tom said. "It's good to see you again, Dr. Spindler, especially when I *don't* have to worry about getting a shot."

"I aim to please," said their visitor.

They squeezed five chairs around the table. Cody ate with gusto, making enough noise and mess to prevent any serious conversation from developing among the adults.

They were nearly finished when Jolene said, "You know, Tom, I've been thinking about your son going up to the attic. I believe it would be best if Cody slept in my room tonight."

"Your room?" Tom gazed at her over the rim of his coffee mug. "Why?"

"If he's going to go roving, it's best to keep him as far from the attic as possible." In the clear morning, Jolene didn't look her seventy-eight years. Her expression was as alert, her features as straight, even the angle of her chin as determined as ever. "Besides, if he wakes up in my room, he can play with the computer.''

Marnie could see her grandmother had fixed on a decision, but it seemed an odd one. ''Where exactly would he sleep?''

''We can move the cot,'' she said. ''My room's bigger, anyway.''

Tom shook his head. ''You need your rest, especially now.''

She waved a slim hand. ''I nap all the time. Sometimes I even wake up at night by myself. And when I do, I don't want to have to worry that this little cutie is prowling around my attic. That would be stressful, wouldn't it, Artie?''

Called upon in this peremptory manner, the doctor stopped shredding his second muffin and said, ''That's true. Worry isn't good for her system.''

''*Sì, sì!*'' cried Cody. ''I want to sleep with Nonna Jola!''

Tom regarded his son dubiously. ''I'm not sure another change is a good idea.''

''Believe me, he'll be well taken care of.'' To Jolene, the matter was settled. ''You can bring the cot down after you wash the dishes.''

Tom sputtered into his coffee and took a moment to recover. ''You're volunteering me, are you?''

''Marnie, show me cat!'' Cody demanded. ''Please?''

She remembered telling him about Miss Lacy. ''I thought she might have been what he saw last night.''

Jolene shook her head. ''She sticks close to the barn. She's in what we used to call an interesting condition.''

"That means she's going to have kittens," Marnie translated.

"Kittens?" Cody's eyes got big.

"You're supposed to get animals fixed, you know," Artie commented. "Too many of 'em running around."

"I thought Miss Lacy *was* fixed," Granny snapped. "One of Mrs. Wheedles's other clients gave her up when he moved away, and that's what he said. She's been here two years and this is her first litter."

"That's because all the other cats around here are neutered," said the doctor. "Haven't you seen that new tomcat, the big white bruiser with one ear half bitten off?"

"Oh, *him!*" Granny said. "I drove him away with the hose and figured he wouldn't come back. Guess my birth control method was ineffective. Well, I'll get the cat spayed after she weans."

Cody was wiggling around in his chair, scarcely able to contain his eagerness. "I can take him to the barn," Marnie offered.

"Thanks." Tom met her gaze levelly. "You've been a good sport about everything. I appreciated your help last night."

She didn't know how to answer. Most of the time she could focus on the lively little boy in front of her and put aside her hurt that Tom hadn't wanted to have a child with her. But not always.

"No problem," she muttered, and took Cody into the hall to fetch their coats.

TOM TRIED TO KEEP BUSY clearing the table, scraping the plates and running hot soapy water into the steel sink, but he wished Jolene and the doctor hadn't gone off to play Scrabble. As usual when he was alone, he began stewing in his own memories, no matter how hard he tried to concentrate on the tasks at hand.

When he'd first been sent to the embassy in Rome, he'd volunteered for any assignment, no matter where it had taken him or how potentially dangerous it might be. Traveling and working long hours circumvented the lingering dark thoughts of childhood.

Cody had brought sunshine into his life. Nevertheless, as Tom had feared, returning to Ryder's Crossing was reopening old wounds.

Driving into town, he'd felt a wave of adolescent anger and insecurity sweep over him. It was annoying, and he didn't want to dwell on it, but some part of him remained the gangly boy whom the in crowd refused to credit for any achievement, no matter how hard earned.

Tom still wasn't sure how the townspeople had gotten the idea he was a tough kid. He'd never stolen or been drunk or painted graffiti on walls. Sure, he'd walked around with a chip on his shoulder, thanks to having a father who alternately ignored and insulted him and a mother who'd fled when he was thirteen, but that wasn't his fault.

Yet the merchants had been quick to suspect him when anything got shoplifted, and the police used to come snooping around for cans of spray paint whenever some rude slogan was discovered on a wall. Marnie had admitted that other parents warned her against befriending him.

Well, he *had* often used bad language before he moved in with Jolene, and his knowledge of etiquette had been somewhere in the caveman range, but that was all. Despite his sullen manner, he'd had a right to be seen for who and what he was, especially after his grades began to improve.

Yesterday he'd felt self-conscious just driving past a police cruiser. As if the cop might stop him out of pure cussedness, as if the people of Ryder's Crossing had been waiting all these years to prove to themselves that Furnell Jakes's son was just like his father.

Small towns meant small minds, Tom supposed. He couldn't imagine raising Cody here.

He didn't realize how wound up he'd become until he clanked a dish against the sink. He shouldn't take out his frustrations on Jolene's dishes, he reflected ruefully, especially since she and Marnie were the only people who'd ever cared about him.

And he cared about them, Tom admitted silently as he set it in the drainer. He missed Marnie more than he would have believed possible, even after four years.

He hoped she would consider coming back with him to Italy. Now that he had a son, perhaps that would satisfy her need for a child.

Cody was resilient and precocious, which made him unusually adaptable to his father's life on the move. Tom had to be true to the man he'd become, and that man was a rover.

He got restless staying in one place too long, and the last thing he needed was a whole brood of kids. That kind of family meant settling down and taking on community responsibilities and enmeshing his life with those of other people. To Tom those weren't bonds; they were chains.

He wanted Marnie back. But she had to accept him for himself and not try to turn him into a conventional husband.

The skillet was clean, and the flatware gleaming, and the dishes stacked to dry. It was time to go see how his son and the woman he loved were getting along.

And whether there was hope for the three of them.

Chapter Six

"Snow goes bye-bye," Cody said sadly as his choppy stride carried him across the front yard. The patches of snow were indeed fading into the brown grass.

"We'll probably have more," Marnie assured him. "Does it snow in Rome?"

He shook his head. He was, she supposed, too young to remember living in Sweden.

Against the charcoal landscape, Cody's blue coat stood out as a defiant splash of color. The presence of the child recast the entire scene, making the trees taller and blacker by comparison and the kitchen garden more forlorn in its winter austerity. As they followed the walkway toward the red barn, their breath made clouds in the air.

The great door of the barn stood ajar. From the interior came the musty smell of hay and a lingering aroma of cattle, although none were housed here at the moment.

Lew Ryan maintained the place in good repair, although it was only during unusually severe winters that he boarded livestock here. Marnie remembered that years ago her parents and grandparents had owned horses as well as cattle, chickens and goats.

It was too bad Cody couldn't experience living on a working farm. There was no substitute for the early-morning thrill of finding a speckled egg or the warm scent of a sleepy cow and the splatter of milk into a bucket.

Marnie had had lots of fun in this barn. One Thanksgiving, she and her cousin Mike had infuriated their parents by sneaking into the hayloft, knocking down a big pile of hay and jumping onto it repeatedly.

They might have been seriously harmed, Uncle Norbert had scolded, and even Marnie's mother had glowered. But Marnie's only regret was that she and Mike had got caught. She'd never found an amusement park ride as exciting as that free fall onto the haystack.

When they stepped inside, Marnie glanced along the feed passage that led straight back, but although the doors of the stalls hung open, she couldn't see the interiors. Then she heard a meow coming from her right.

From the direction of the tack room strolled a gin-ger-striped cat. She meowed again and paused to study Cody.

"*Il gato!*" said Cody. "Cat!"

"Yes. She must be hungry." Reaching onto a shelf, Marnie removed a sack of dry cat food and scooped some into the metal dish on the floor. Miss Lacy sniffed it daintily before eating.

The cat's swollen body hung low to the ground, obviously full of kittens. It was an odd time of year to be having a litter, Marnie reflected, but she wouldn't expect a pet belonging to her grandmother to do anything the conventional way.

When Miss Lacy took a break from eating, Marnie knelt and scratched behind the cat's ears. Purrs rumbled into the air.

Cody also crouched and reached cautiously to touch the ginger fur, not making any unnecessary noise. For such a young child, he had a lot of self-control.

A born diplomat? No wonder Tom found the child suited to his way of life.

As she petted Miss Lacy, Marnie noted that the coat was thick and soft. Through it, her palm made contact with the cat's swollen side, and she felt something ripple and seethe.

So this was how babies felt inside their mother, she realized with a rush of longing. She didn't want to think about what it would be like to carry a baby of her own. The possibility seemed so wonderful and so unattainable that it made her ache.

"She's fat." Cody pointed to the low-slung belly.

"It's kittens," Marnie said. "Here, feel."

His hesitation turned to wonder as he pressed his palm against Miss Lacy's side. It rose and fell visibly as the kittens churned.

"Can they come out and play?" he asked.

"Soon." It seemed too much to hope that the birth would occur by Sunday, though. "If you're gone, I'll send you photos."

The cat, having finished its breakfast, rubbed against Cody's leg. "She likes me," he said.

"Yes, she does."

"She doesn't bite?"

"Not unless you hurt her." Marnie believed that many animals knew the difference between adult humans and children. Some even displayed a maternal protectiveness and would gentle their actions around a little one.

Just like her, she realized. She'd reacted that way to Cody instantly, and to a lesser degree she had the same tender feeling toward these soon-to-be-born kittens.

For one risky moment she let herself speculate. What if she and Tom were married and she were the one carrying new life inside?

How would it feel, to touch her abdomen and feel a tiny foot or elbow? She envisioned Tom's hand against her pregnant belly, sharing the miracle they had created together.

Would the child have his blue eyes or Marnie's brown ones? Blond hair or brunette? Maybe it would be a little girl.

Her eyes filled suddenly. Marnie barely had time to blink back the tears before she heard masculine footsteps and looked up to see Tom in the doorway.

He stood silhouetted against the weak sunlight, studying her and Cody. "Communing with nature?"

"Kitties." Cody pointed at Miss Lacy.

Outside, a car started, and Marnie realized Artie must be leaving. "I need to say goodbye."

Tom stood with legs braced, his body half blocking the great door. Marnie wondered wildly if he meant to tackle her should she attempt to leave, and then Cody broke the standoff by dashing between his father's legs.

"Hey!" Tom swung around, and Marnie seized the chance to edge by him into the yard.

He joined her to say farewell to Artie and make sure Cody stayed clear of the four-wheel-drive vehicle. The boy bounced around like Tigger until the doctor puttered away, then announced, "I'm hungry!"

"Let's go have a snack." Granny took the boy's arm. "Tom, Marnie, it's time for you to decorate."

"The tree's done," Marnie reminded her.

"I don't mean that!" said Jolene. "We've got to get the house decked out. I mean to show this boy what a real down-home Christmas is like."

"I spotted the outdoor lights in one of the boxes," Tom said. "The brackets are still attached above the porch. It won't take long to put them up."

Marnie nearly countered that she could put up decorations herself, thank you. But that would be foolish, she decided, since Tom was considerably taller than her five-foot-three-inch frame.

"Fine," she said. "I'll get started on some baking."

"You'll do no such thing." Halfway to the house, her grandmother swung to face them. "I'm not having this man fall off a shaky ladder because you weren't there to steady it!"

"If the ladder's not sturdy, there's not much I'll be able to do about it," Marnie said.

"Well, somebody has to hold the lights and feed them to me. I've only got two hands," Tom countered.

She was trapped. If only Uncle Norbert or Cousin

Mike were here, she could insist that they do the job. But until they arrived, Marnie was stuck with Tom.

"Well, if you insist," she grumbled. "Let's hurry up, then."

TOM HADN'T REALLY BELIEVED he needed help putting up lights. He'd done it half a dozen times before, winding the rope of lights around his shoulders and balancing easily on the ladder.

Once he got the aluminum ladder angled and anchored, however, he discovered that he'd lost some of his kinesthetic sense. Mastering diplomatic protocol, making security arrangements for VIP visitors and dealing with the press were no substitute for the rigors of doing repair work around the farmhouse or working out on the rings in gymnastics.

He decided not to get as elaborate with the decorations as he'd done one year in college, when he created a giant five-point star. A continuous strand that traced the perimeter of the porch would be fine.

Marnie did her best to ignore him as she waited beside the ladder, the pale sunshine bringing out a hint of russet in her hair. When he asked for something, she thrust it at him, and when he deliberately made the ladder quake, she gripped it without looking at him.

What had put her in such a rotten mood? Tom wondered as he unsnarled a length of multicolored bulbs. He must have pushed one of her emotional buttons.

Could it mean she regretted their breakup?

The woman was incredibly obstinate. She had to be as aware as he was that they belonged together. The emotions that had sparked between them as teenagers showed no sign of dimming; in fact, their need for each other had grown over the years. So why not yield to the inevitable?

He knew that having a stepson wasn't the same as giving birth, but Marnie obviously liked Cody. And, while she was attached to Ryder's Crossing, she'd left it to be with Tom once before.

To his logical mind her behavior simply didn't make sense. Perhaps he hadn't made his position clear.

Tom began stringing lights on the left side of the porch, then moved to the right, in front of the parlor. By now, Jolene and Cody must be either eating in the kitchen or playing computer games in her bedroom, and thus safely out of earshot. He could speak openly.

"You know, I've never blamed you for leaving," he began.

No response. A couple of crows sitting on a telephone wire appeared to fascinate Marnie.

"We always had a lot of fun together," he continued.

"What's your point?" The words rapped out like bursts of buckshot.

Tom chuckled in spite of himself. "How's a fellow supposed to get romantic with a drill sergeant?"

Her face tilted toward him. "You're trying to get romantic ten feet up a ladder?"

"See how desperate I am?"

Amusement warred with annoyance on her face. "I don't know why you're joking about this."

"Neither do I," he admitted, "except that I like to see you smile."

She frowned. "You do?"

"I think we have a communication gap here. Just a minute." Tom wanted to get rid of the rest of the lights in a hurry, so, although he really should have moved the ladder one more time, he leaned out to drape them onto the final set of hooks.

Bad idea. The ground below had turned soggy from melting snow, and his sudden shift of weight threw the ladder to one side. It swayed alarmingly.

Marnie grabbed the side rails, but the stepladder was reaching a dangerous angle and the last thing Tom wanted was to fall on top of her. "Move!"

Stubbornly, she held on. "Climb down!"

"You're in the way!"

"I'll move back when you get here! Hurry!"

He descended a rung, which only increased the trajectory of the wobble. One of the braces hadn't locked properly; he'd noticed earlier that it was loose, but it had seemed to snap into place. Now it formed an inverted V and, even as he debated what to do next, he felt the whole apparatus giving way.

To Tom, events passed in slow motion: Marnie's look of alarm, her step backward, his frantic attempt to bodily guide the ladder away from her.

Afterward Tom wasn't sure how he managed it, but by spreading his legs and pressing the edges of his shoes into the side rails, he was able to slide down while maintaining the ladder in a state of shaky suspension. He landed in a narrow space—very narrow—between Marnie and the rungs.

The shock of hitting the ground reverberated through his leg bones. So did the tension of discovering his ex-wife's body so close behind his that her breath tickled his neck.

Her hips rubbed his thighs and her breasts pressed against his back. Despite their heavy coats, Tom found himself hypersensitive to her touch.

"You okay?" he asked, trying to see her over his shoulder.

"Oof," came the response.

"You can let go of me," he said. "I've got the ladder steady."

She didn't move. "You scared me."

"You're not hurt, though?"

"You're standing on my foot," she said. "Could you get off it, please?"

He wriggled a few inches, but she held on to the ladder, which meant her arms remained wrapped around him. Tom decided he was in no hurry to be released.

Her cheek came to rest between his shoulder blades. Despite a bit of weakness in the knees, he had more than enough energy left to kiss her, he judged, but only a contortionist could have managed it at this angle.

"I've heard of men getting killed falling off ladders." Her voice quavered.

"I was never in any serious danger," he demurred, although it wasn't quite true. "An old gymnast like me?"

"Not to mention your hard head," she grumped. "What did you think you were doing, leaning over that way?"

"Saving time."

"This is your idea of a shortcut?"

The breeze was chilling his bare hands, and having his face practically pushed into the rungs wasn't exactly Tom's idea of a good time. However, when he glanced upward, he saw that he had indeed managed to snag the lights over the hook. ''Well, it worked.''

''By whose definition?'' Slowly, as if afraid he might crumple, she eased back.

When Tom turned, he saw that her face was ashen. ''You were worried about me,'' he said. ''Or were you afraid I'd knock you over?''

She pushed back a hank of brown hair. ''You knocked out my hair comb.''

''You weren't wearing one.''

''Oh.'' She tucked her hair behind her ear. ''Well, no harm done except to our nerves. We'll have to get that ladder repaired.''

''I'll do it later.'' The one skill Tom had learned from his father was how to fix things, since Furnell had earned his intermittent income as a handyman. ''First we need to assess the damage. Starting with an inspection.''

''Sure.'' She didn't catch his drift until he seized her upper arms and scrutinized her at close range. ''Hey!''

''You might be in shock,'' he advised. ''We need to warm you.''

Without waiting for permission, which would never come anyway, he caught her mouth in a kiss. A soft gasp escaped her, but she didn't pull away.

He drew her closer. She tasted of cinnamon and sunshine, and she clung to him as if she, too, felt this welling hunger.

Vaguely Tom noted that they were standing in front of the house in full view of—well, there was no one around, was there? Besides, surely there must be some mistletoe hanging from the eaves, or something that could pass for mistletoe in a pinch.

Their coats might cushion their upper-body contact, but their jeans virtually became a second skin. He felt the pulse in her body, and his own throbbing response.

What were they doing, living halfway around the world from each other? He doubted anyone, anywhere, had ever been more married than they were.

His fingers slipped through the back of Marnie's hair, guiding her head as he deepened the kiss. Judging by her low moan, she needed little encouragement.

Inside his coat, his cell phone rang. *Go away,* Tom thought as it sounded a second time.

"Don't you have to answer that?" Marnie asked thickly, coming up for air.

"It's probably nothing. World War III breaking out or something," he muttered.

"Tom!"

The mood was broken, so he reached inside his coat and yanked the phone from his shirt pocket. His numb fingers had trouble pressing the right button, so two more rings sounded before he got it to his ear.

"Tom Jakes," he said.

"Sorry to disturb you." It was Norbert. "I didn't want to call on Mother Jolene's line in case she was sleeping, and I figured she gave me this number for a reason."

"*She* gave you this number?" Tom repeated. "I guess she wanted to make sure we wouldn't miss your call even if we went somewhere."

"They're resuming flights out of O'Hare, but the

backup is tremendous,'' the minister continued in his dry, slightly nasal tone. ''We'd prefer not to catch a red-eye special, so Linda and I are booked on a flight just before noon tomorrow. We'll rent a car, as planned, so look for us around dinnertime. Is Mike there yet?''

''He had some car trouble,'' Tom said. ''We haven't heard anything today.''

''He should have had it serviced before he left Santa Fe, but he never plans in advance,'' Norbert said. ''Let's hope it's minor.''

They uttered the usual civilities about looking forward to seeing each other and hung up.

''More delays?'' Marnie asked.

''They'll arrive Christmas Eve around dinnertime.'' Tom weighed the chances of resuming their interrupted activity, and, based on the fact that his ex-wife was heading for the porch, estimated them at zero. ''What's next on the agenda?''

''Lunch,'' she said. ''Then we need to make Granny's sugar cookies.''

''I vote for refrigerator dough,'' he offered as they went into the house.

''I hope you're joking,'' she said. ''You know how particular she is about following her mother's recipe.''

Tom had to admit that although at first he'd wondered why anyone would go to so much trouble for something that would disappear in minutes, he'd grown to treasure the buttery taste and inviting shapes and colors of Jolene's decorated cookies. Making them wasn't a chore, it was an art form.

In the front hall he removed his coat and hung it

beside Marnie's. She had already disappeared into the kitchen.

He knew there was no chance of getting his arms around her again for the next hour or so, but he wasn't giving up hope. Norbert wouldn't be here for more than twenty-four hours. As for her cousin Mike's car, he silently and with only a twinge of guilt wished for it to stay broken one more day.

Now Tom just had to bide his time and seize his chance.

Chapter Seven

For Marnie, the buttery-vanilla scent of baking cookies carried sweet memories of Christmases past. With
each breath, she inhaled the years of her childhood,
the people she had loved and the casual happiness she
had once taken for granted.

As she washed the cookie cutters and mixing bowls
in the sink, she wished that time could be elastic. It
should be possible, if she wished hard enough, to become once more a seven-year-old thrilled by the gift
of a stuffed panda, or a nine-year-old eating candied
yams at the dining room table while her parents and
grandparents discussed politics.

Marnie had lived in this house since birth. It was
Artie Spindler himself who had delivered her in an
upstairs bedroom after her mother, with typical stoi-
cism, delayed too long to get to a hospital.

Her father, Nicholas Afton, had helped his parents
run the farm. Her mother, Mary Anne, had come from
a family of old-time barnstormers and stunt pilots, and
even after Marnie was born she continued to fly a
small plane based at a nearby landing strip.

The two had been so devoted they named their

daughter for each other. "Marnie" was a blend of Mary Anne and Nicholas.

She retained only fragmented memories of her parents. Her father smelled like hay, her mother like brownies and diesel oil. She remembered her father bringing her mother a bunch of wildflowers, and her mother throwing her arms around him in joyful abandon.

Mary Anne had piloted friends and neighbors when they needed to go somewhere in an emergency. She'd also flown for pleasure, saying she never felt as free as when she floated on clouds.

The crash had occurred during a sudden thunderstorm, while her parents were en route to an agricultural show. A lightning strike, Granny had said. For Marnie, the discovery that life was precarious had ripped her world apart. It had also taught her to seize happiness wherever she found it.

So, years later, when Tom asked her to marry him, she jumped at the chance, even though she sensed he held a part of himself in reserve. She had hoped that time and love would open the doors.

Well, someone else had succeeded where Marnie had failed. But she couldn't feel resentment toward Cody's mother. It wasn't her fault, or anyone's, that she'd borne the child Marnie longed for.

Besides, Marnie had a task to carry out, one that she couldn't put off any longer. As she dried the mixing bowls, she glanced over to where Tom sat icing a plate of bell-shaped cookies.

Domestic work had never been his favorite, yet he handled it with grace and precision. As she watched, he manipulated the butter knife to create a delicate swirl.

She cleared her throat, preparing to speak. At the sound his hand jerked and the cookie broke in two.

"Sorry," Marnie said.

"I think I'll survive." With a wink, he popped the pieces into his mouth. "What are you going to tackle next? Don't tell me you're finished!"

"There's one more batch in the oven. Also, Granny asked me to make a fruitcake, but I don't know if I should. It can't be good for her heart." Granny's recipe wasn't exactly heart healthy. "It's more like a fat and sugar loaf with a little fruit in it."

"Sounds perfect." Tom grinned.

"Do they make fruitcakes in Italy?" Going to the recipe box, she took out the card.

"Sure. They call it *panettone,* which means 'big bread.' There's a little fruit and a lot of bread, slightly sweet. It's traditional at New Year's." He finished icing the last cookie. "Well, I'm done here. I think I'll make more coffee."

As she fetched the ingredients from the pantry, Marnie decided she'd procrastinated long enough. In what she hoped was a casual tone, she said, "Have you ever thought about leaving the Foreign Service?"

He didn't answer. When she turned, she saw Tom poised with a beaker of water in his hand as if he'd forgotten it was there.

"Well?" she prompted.

"Is there some reason for your question?" Noticing the water at last, he poured it into the coffeemaker.

"Does there have to be?" That was hardly fair,

since she *did* have an ulterior motive, so she added, "I was wondering if you'd ever considered doing anything else. I mean, it has been nearly ten years."

From the time he'd attended a career fair during college and learned that a man could serve his country working in distant parts of the globe, Tom had never considered any other path. Although Marnie would have preferred to live closer to her grandmother, she'd accepted that there was no alternative for Tom.

But that was a decade ago. Now he had a son, and had reached a point in his career at which people often experienced second thoughts about moving from country to country every few years.

"I did get an offer about a year ago," he said. "A U.S. manufacturer expanding into Italy had contacted the embassy for assistance. I answered their questions and referred them to an attorney who could help negotiate the red tape. Their CEO offered me a job at more than double what I make."

"What kind of job?" Marnie asked.

He glanced down as the coffeemaker hissed and began dripping brown liquid into the carafe. "I know what I should buy for Granny. An espresso machine."

"One of those things that sounds like a 747 taking off?" she said. "Great idea. She can use it to scare skunks from nesting under the house. Now, what kind of job?"

Tom tapped his fingers against the counter. "Oh, vice president in charge of paper shuffling, something like that. They just wanted an American guy who spoke Italian and had contacts in the business community."

He made it sound like no big deal, but she suspected the CEO had been impressed by Tom's take-charge professionalism. The irony was that, despite all his accomplishments, her ex-husband still didn't realize how highly he was regarded.

Marnie had read once that people tended to get stuck with adolescent images of themselves. That was certainly true of Tom, perhaps because his youth had been so traumatic.

"I think you're selling yourself short," she said.

"Maybe." He shrugged. "Anyway, the hours were long and they had the option of transferring me to their headquarters in Virginia. I want to stay overseas."

"As far from Ryder's Crossing as you can get?" she blurted.

His gaze met hers. "You could say that."

Oh, wonderful. Without even asking what she wanted to know, Marnie had received her answer.

She had hoped that, despite his unpleasant memories of their school years, the emotional sting might have faded. But Tom had made it clear that old hurts still rankled.

He would never come back. Not for her, not for Cody's sake, not even for Granny. This brief holiday visit was the most he could offer.

"Are you trying to make a point?" he asked.

Marnie paused in the middle of greasing a small loaf pan. "Excuse me?"

"I keep getting the sense there's a purpose behind your questions."

He was hitting too close to the truth. "Isn't being your old friend reason enough to wonder what you plan to do with the rest of your life?" she countered.

He poured himself a cup of coffee. "Well, I appreciate your interest. While we're on the subject, what do you want from the rest of your life, Marnie?"

She hadn't been prepared for him to turn the tables. It wasn't as if *he* had an offer to make. The answer, though, seemed obvious. "What I've always wanted, I guess."

The timer beeped. Tom grabbed the potholders and took out the last batch of cookies, this time in star shapes. After kneeing the oven door shut, he set them on the cooktop. "And what would that be?"

"Kids. A husband. A place where I belong." She measured several cups of candied fruit into a bowl.

"Such as Ryder's Crossing?"

The past four years, she'd put down roots here as an adult, which was very different from simply growing up in a place. She'd made an investment in the town, yet that didn't mean she could never leave it. "Not necessarily. But I like it here, yes."

He straddled a chair, his mouth twisting with irony. "Isn't it odd how two people can grow up together and be so different?"

"I suppose it is." She wondered if she should present the proposition, anyway, but she was feeling too vulnerable to risk an outright rejection.

It was a relief when Cody ran in and demanded to go for a walk. He and Tom set off together, and Marnie took out her jumpiness by stirring the fruitcake batter so hard it made her arm ache.

DR. SPINDLER RETURNED at dinnertime, per Granny's invitation. He assisted his patient, who claimed she was feeling a mite weak, into the dining room, where

Marnie had set out cold cuts, cheeses, bread, potato salad and a vegetable tray on the sideboard. She'd also arranged a selection of desserts.

Her cousin Mike had called to say that his car needed work on the brakes, and that if it couldn't be finished by tomorrow he'd have to catch a bus. At least he didn't suggest hitchhiking as he once would have, Marnie reflected.

She smiled as Tom, ahead of her in the buffet line, built the world's strangest sandwich for his son. No meat or cheese, just tomatoes, black olives, and—at Cody's insistence—a thin slice of fruitcake.

"Well, why not?" Tom regarded his creation with reluctant admiration. "When else in his life is he going to get exactly what he wants?"

"I hope he wants a stomachache, because he's going to get one!" Granny said tartly. "Don't forget, he's sleeping in *my* room."

"The kid has a stomach of cast iron," Tom assured her.

Marnie fixed herself some corned beef on rye, with Swiss cheese and mustard. It seemed dull by comparison.

She took a seat next to Granny and wondered why, during his phone call, her cousin had used the pronoun "we" a couple of times. When she asked if he was bringing someone, he'd muttered "Well, gotta go," and hung up.

"What's going on with Mike?" she asked Jolene. "Is he bringing a friend?"

"A small surprise," she said, and turned toward the doctor, a clear indication that she didn't intend to explain, either. Her grandmother loved playing little tricks, and so did Mike, Marnie mused.

They'd known each other well during their childhoods, when Uncle Norbert headed a church in Ryder's Crossing. Although three years younger than Marnie, her red-haired cousin had displayed twice the energy and ten times the mischief.

Unfortunately, as he grew, he chafed under his father's restrictions. In high school Mike ran away several times and only graduated by the skin of his teeth.

There followed a series of odd jobs in various locations, times when he disappeared entirely, and one kooky girlfriend after another. According to Jolene, he'd settled in Santa Fe last year and landed a steady job managing a music store.

The last time Marnie had seen him was three years ago at Thanksgiving, when he'd appeared at the farmhouse unannounced. Scraggly red hair hung halfway down his back, and his clothes were patched, but he'd been full of his usual lively humor.

"Will Babbo Natale come tonight?" Cody asked between bites of sandwich.

"Tomorrow night," Tom said. "That's Santa Claus, in English."

"Santa Claus," the boy repeated through a mouthful of food.

"Don't talk with your mouth full," Jolene said briskly. "Especially when it's full of that bizarre concoction."

"How is it?" Artie asked.

"Good." Cody took another bite.

"Maybe I should make one for myself." Tom

sneaked a sideways glance at Jolene, waiting for her to protest.

Instead she said, "Go ahead. There's plenty left."

He chuckled. "I just might."

"Are we giving odds?" Marnie asked.

"Tomato, olive and fruitcake," said the doctor, joining the teasing. "That might taste good on pizza, too."

He made a little jerking motion, and Marnie got the impression he'd been kicked under the table. Her grandmother, however, calmly continued eating her potato salad.

After dinner they adjourned to the living room, where Jolene settled into her antique rocker and Dr. Spindler made himself comfortable on an embroidered settee. With Cody tagging along, Tom fetched a couple of logs in a canvas carrier and set to work building a fire.

Soon a blaze sent red and yellow sparks snapping into the air, and he fixed the fire screen firmly in place. Around the room, the four adults relaxed. Even Cody seemed mellower than usual as he pored over a floor jigsaw puzzle, a fire engine cut into a half-dozen large pieces.

The tang of burning wood blended with the scent of pine from the Christmas tree to give Marnie a deep sense of contentment. From beneath lowered lashes, she saw Tom lean forward on his straight chair, wearing a bemused expression. Then she realized he was watching her.

Glow from the fire warmed his lightly tanned face and brought out a sparkle in his blue eyes. She missed him so much it hurt, even though he was sitting right there.

Was he remembering past times together, or simply enjoying the moment? Even after knowing him for eighteen years, she couldn't tell what he wanted from her.

At times his manner toward her seemed tender and even flirtatious. He'd kissed her twice, and not just casual pecks, either.

Yet he didn't intend to live in Ryder's Crossing; and he'd made it plain that he didn't want more children. What he sought, she supposed, was what he'd had before: fun and companionship. But she needed so much more.

"I had the piano tuned last month," Jolene observed into the crackling silence. "I don't suppose anyone would care to play it."

It was her way of prompting her granddaughter. An invitation to disaster, in Marnie's opinion, but she'd anticipated this development and practiced on the piano at church.

"I suppose a few carols wouldn't hurt." Rising from her chair, she went to open the keyboard on the carved upright.

A book of Christmas songs was strategically displayed on the music rack. Marnie turned to her favorite, "White Christmas."

Her soft soprano didn't carry far, but soon it was joined by her grandmother's dry tones and Artie's gruff ones. Then Tom's rich baritone vibrated through the room, making her shiver with an emotion she couldn't identify.

Just let us stay like this forever. Even if he couldn't

be her husband, even if she would never have his child, let them live suspended in this moment with their voices filling the night.

Marnie segued into one song after another. Cody joined in, piping up with vague imitations of the words and notes, somehow enriching the effect.

She would have liked to go on playing all night, but after a half-dozen songs, her fingers started to ache, and Cody was yawning. Jolene's head nodded a couple of times, as well.

Reluctantly Marnie stopped. "Sleepy time."

Tom nodded reluctantly and picked up his drooping son. Surely the time difference and jet lag must be wearing on him, too, she thought, but he didn't show it.

Artie helped Jolene to her feet. "I'll drop by tomorrow afternoon. We've got to finish that Scrabble game," he said. "But I don't think I can come for dinner. Tomorrow night I'm serving dinner at the senior citizens center. Plus I'm on call while Doc Rosen's out of town for the holiday."

"Well, there's always room for you here if you change your mind." Although Jolene's voice was strong, she leaned on the doctor's arm as they went into the hallway, and Marnie hoped she wasn't overtired.

"Let's go bring down your pajamas and toothbrush," Tom told Cody. "You're sleeping with Nonna Jola, remember?"

"Okay." The little boy rubbed his eyes.

As the others departed, Marnie wondered if it was wise for her and Tom to stay alone on the second floor, even though their rooms were at opposite ends.

There was a foldout couch downstairs in the sewing room, but after a moment's consideration she decided it would look ridiculous if she insisted on staying there.

As if she didn't trust Tom. As if she didn't trust herself.

Neither of them was going to seduce the other. Besides, she was exhausted. No doubt she would sleep soundly all night, without interruptions from door-knocking cats or mysterious, disappearing angels.

DESPITE HIS WEARINESS Tom lay awake picturing Marnie as she sat at the piano, and hearing her sweet voice once again. This was what Christmas meant to him, being with her and Jolene and Cody, being a family. But the things he and Marnie wanted from life simply weren't compatible.

He wondered why the differences between them hadn't surfaced earlier. Was it because as long as they both lived in Ryder's Crossing, she didn't have to deal with the side of him that needed movement and change?

Yet she'd moved to Knoxville with him to attend the University of Tennessee instead of going to college closer to home. And she'd married him with the knowledge that it meant living abroad.

He tossed between the cool sheets and pressed his cheek into the pillow. It smelled of Jolene's familiar laundry soap; he hadn't realized how much he missed that scent.

He wanted Marnie to come to Rome with him, but this business of children appeared to be holding her back. He wished he could convey how difficult it had been for him when he first learned about Cody and realized he would have to give the boy a home.

Tom had found himself awakening at night, in near panic. He'd felt trapped, the same as he had when his mother'd left him alone with his father.

He still couldn't believe how easily Cody had snuggled into his life. Perhaps it had been because Tom needed someone to help fill the emptiness left by Marnie's defection. Also, the boy was unusually adaptable, a good traveler who rarely fussed.

Tom kept trying to find a rational explanation for the cornered feeling he got whenever he thought about having more children, especially since he knew how much Marnie wanted them. For him, emotions had never been easy to define.

Mostly he needed his wife to love him for himself. Not because he fit into some preconceived role, not because she could make him into someone else, but for himself, Tom Jakes. A man in charge of his own life, independent and free to live in the wide world.

However, in the wide world there was only one woman he'd ever loved, or ever would. Somehow he had to find a way to make her understand that.

He must have dozed, because it was 1:00 a.m. when Tom's eyes snapped open. Maybe his body clock had awakened him, he reflected sleepily; it was, after all, 8:00 a.m. in Rome.

Then he heard a rustling in the hall.

''Cody?'' He swung out of bed. Receiving no response, he pulled a robe over his pajamas, stuck his feet into loafers and grabbed a flashlight.

Chapter Eight

Hurrying toward the stairs, Tom spotted a silhouette halfway up. "Who's there?"

His flashlight revealed Marnie's worried frown. "I heard something in the attic. I thought it might be Cody."

At bedtime Tom had helped Granny hang a chime above her door so his son couldn't exit without rousing her. "Probably a raccoon."

"Whatever it is, I'd like to figure out how it's getting in."

Tom couldn't think about raccoons at the moment. He was too busy noticing the way Marnie's robe and nightgown clung to her feminine shape and, as he got closer, the sleep-softened dewiness of her face that made him long to curve his palm around her cheek and bring her mouth to his.

This was dangerous territory. Tightening his robe belt, he said, "Let's go."

"Do you think it's wise? I mean, for us to be alone up there?" her voice quavered.

Tom refused to concede to any weakness, even after the way they'd embraced in front of the house in broad daylight. "I'm sure we can handle it," he said.

"I guess so," Marnie said dubiously, and swung around.

As they climbed, he tried in vain not to react to the gentle sway of her hips. This was his wife, the woman with whom he'd first experienced intimacy.

He had a photograph of her racing along the beach in Hawaii on their honeymoon, her long, brown hair flowing above the flowered swimsuit. She'd been laughing as she came toward him.

There was, of course, no picture of what happened next. Tom had swept her into his arms and carried her to their hotel room, ignoring the amused glances of onlookers.

He'd kicked the door shut behind them. Lowering her to the bed, he'd stripped the suit from her damp, eager body....

"Tom?" She stood poised at the top of the stairs.

"You check to the left. I'll take the right. Use your flashlight." He didn't want to switch on the chandelier and send their target scampering for cover.

The two beams fanned across the moonlit maze of trunks and cabinets. The draped furniture loomed like shapes in an alien landscape, but Tom didn't spot any movement.

Near the rear wall, something creaked, like a board beneath someone's foot. A chill ran down his spine.

Marnie drew closer. "What's that?"

Resting one hand on her waist, he kept the flashlight trained ahead. "Who's there?" he called.

His voice echoed through the cavernous space.

Then the weight of the floor shifted, as if someone or something had moved.

"Did you feel that?"

"Yes," she whispered.

He listened harder, but detected nothing more. Were they letting their imaginations run away with them? Tom wondered.

Then a sound came, a low rasp from the back of the attic. Moving in front of Marnie, he made a rapid survey of the open spaces, but nothing scurried as a frightened animal might do.

"This doesn't make sense," he said. "I really don't see how it can be a burglar, three stories up with the windows locked."

"Someone could have broken in downstairs," Marnie said.

"He'd have gone for the presents under the tree, not come up here and risk getting trapped." Beyond the storage cabinets, Tom spotted a closet door. He found it locked. "What's in here?"

Marnie regarded it with a faraway expression. "Gee, I'd forgotten all about that."

"About what?" Even as he asked, Tom remembered seeing similar doors near the rear of the first and second floors. He'd assumed they were closets.

"It's an old staircase," she said. "For servants, I guess. It's steep and narrow."

"Why is it locked?" Tom said. "I don't recall anyone using it when I lived here."

"Mike rolled marbles down it one Thanksgiving and made us all jump out of our skins." Marnie chuckled. "Granny was afraid one of us kids would fall down it someday and break our necks, so she made Grandpa lock it.''

Tom tried the door again. ''Well, it feels solid. I don't see how anyone could have sneaked out that way.''

They toured the attic once more, but there was nothing amiss. ''A raccoon could have made those noises,'' Tom said. ''There must be a small opening hidden behind one of these boxes. I'll look for it tomorrow.''

Marnie paused before a mirror. ''This is where Cody and I saw the rainbow.''

Standing behind her, Tom couldn't resist brushing his cheek against her hair. She smelled of spring flowers.

Then he saw a shimmer of colors in the glass. It had to be moonlight filtering through the chandelier, he told himself, yet there was a kind of magic about the way it appeared from nowhere.

''Fantastic,'' he said.

''When I was little, Mom and I would come up here to picnic,'' Marnie said. ''I used to believe this place was enchanted.''

''Maybe it is.'' In the mirror Tom saw his arms wrap around her. ''Now we're part of the magic,'' he murmured.

She leaned back against his chest. ''You belong here,'' she said. ''With me.''

''We belong together,'' he corrected. ''It doesn't have to be here.''

''What other place has magic mirrors?''

''We make our own magic,'' he said, ''wherever we go.''

With a deep sigh she nestled against him. Engulfed in faerie colors, the man in the mirror shifted the woman to face him and gazed down at her in wonder and collected her in his embrace.

Tom lost track of their images in the mirror as warmth and longing enveloped him. Marnie felt very real, her lips parting to admit his tongue and her skin warm beneath his touch.

He told himself they shouldn't be doing this, and then couldn't summon up a single reason why not. This was his wife, his other self. Their divorce meant less than nothing. ...*let no man put asunder*.

Marnie slipped her hands inside his robe to his bare chest beneath. A moment later her mouth played across his chest.

Primal heat tightened his masculine core and urged him to take her here, now, on this hard floor with the spectrum of colors playing across their naked skin. Instead, he held himself rigidly in check as her tongue traced a line of fire down his stomach.

All his wildness belonged to Marnie. And despite her outwardly reserved manner, he had discovered long ago that she guarded a sensuality that only he could unleash.

She traced a whorl around his navel before rising to claim his mouth. A groan tore from him, ragged with years of pent-up need. Seizing her hips, he pulled her tight, plundered her mouth and lost himself in her silken invitation.

With the last presence of mind he could summon, Tom guided her across the floor toward the stairs. For one flicker of an instant, he saw that other couple in the mirror, their faces flushed with passion as they disappeared into the mists of their own private universe. Then they were gone.

FOR FOUR YEARS Marnie had denied her need for a man. For this man, for Tom.

She didn't know where she'd found the boldness to loosen his robe and probe his chest. She'd felt arousal harden his muscles, and his masculine core. It gave her a delicious sense of power.

But she was also skating on a knife-edge of her own desire. Tom held the same power over her, and she wanted him to use it.

As they reached the second floor, he stopped in a ray of moonlight that shone through the hall window. His open robe revealed a muscular torso, reminding Marnie of a Greek statue she'd seen once in a museum.

This was her conquering hero. She hoped he wouldn't ask if this was what she really wanted; for one night, Marnie refused to think about consequences.

Then he caught her hands in his and pulled her toward his room. His eyes flashed blue fire as they entered.

Gazing up at the hard planes of his face, she saw that the last traces of boyishness had vanished. In many ways this man was a stranger to her.

A stranger who knew her intimately. Knew her weaknesses and her needs and didn't hesitate to seat her on the bed beside him.

Strong hands slipped the nightgown down her shoulders, and his thumbs raised peaks on her breasts. Curling against him, Marnie inhaled the musky tang of his arousal and knew that she wanted this fierce marauder, wanted to tame him and be possessed by him.

Tom stroked her neck, touched her earlobes, tangled his hands through her hair. He tilted her face and kissed her, long and lovingly.

Then his mouth trailed down to her breasts, and he lowered her across the bed. Cool air rushed in as he withdrew, but quickly he returned, unrolling protection over himself.

"You came prepared?" she asked, half offended, half amused.

"In the Foreign Service we have to be on the alert at all times." Before she could respond, he cupped her breasts and bent to taste the nipples. Desire shocked through her, driving out any other thought.

She would not yield so easily. Not without prolonging the anticipation, rubbing one leg along his, pressing upward so that her breasts danced against his chest. Nibbling his lips and cheek and chin, dodging his attempts to capture her in another kiss.

As he arched over her, Marnie couldn't resist stroking his corded thighs and the strong back poised over her. The powerful muscles of his buttocks tightened, ready to thrust.

She was burning, but she wanted to touch the essence of him, to feel him come alive in her hand and hear the guttural longing break from his throat. And she did, caressing him until she knew he must be nearing his peak.

When she released him, Tom's mouth met hers, almost roughly. At the same time he stroked her legs apart, found her core with his thumb and tantalized it to a knot of yearning.

His manhood made its home inside her with a long slow entry and then a hard push. She wrapped her arms around him and felt a shudder run from his jaw all the way to his groin.

Without warning she pulled away, ducked aside, twisted and pushed Tom down beneath her. The loss of his fierce possession ached, but only for a moment. Then she swung her leg over him and straddled him.

He pushed straight up into her, like a wild stallion who could be ridden only at his own pleasure. And pleasure he took, fierce and wonderful, until his feral nature invaded hers and made them one in spirit as well as in flesh.

He was in her, around her, carrying her up to the stars as a burst of pure joy enveloped them both.

The climax ebbed slowly. Tom rolled away for a moment, and then he gathered her close. "Come here."

She lay against his shoulder, fulfilled, happy. Wanting to stay there forever and think of nothing.

Tom dozed beside her, his breathing slow and satisfied. Her Tom. No, not hers. Not completely. There was a part of him she hardly knew, and perhaps never would.

Nothing mattered except tonight. For this brief time their closeness wiped away all the pain and the doubt.

She would take what happiness she could. For however long it lasted.

MARNIE AWOKE with the pleasant sense that all was right with the world. It took her a moment to sort out that she lay in Tom's bed and that her body hummed with a satisfaction she hadn't felt in years.

The mismatched furnishings testified to the fact that this was a guest room. The chenille quilt: a gift from a neighbor that hadn't quite suited Granny's taste. The painted china lamp with bows around the shade: an impulsive purchase Marnie had made at an estate sale. The aging rose-patterned wallpaper: a reminder of former times, left in place because the blinds were rarely opened and so it faded less than elsewhere.

Yet the room was far from impersonal. How could it be, with the electricity of lovemaking still pervading the air?

Rolling over, she saw that Tom lay on his back, his muscular chest gleaming in the morning light. It struck her again that he was all man now, without a hint of the awkward, angry boy she'd known.

Humor glinted in his eyes. "Happy, Mrs. Jakes?"

His use of her married name startled Marnie, but she decided to let it pass. "Yes. And a little stunned, I guess."

Tom reached over to brush a strand of hair from her temple. "Last night was wonderful. Did I mention that?"

"We didn't do a lot of talking," she admitted.

He lifted himself on one elbow. "I didn't tell you that your lips are like rose petals and your skin is like silk?"

"I think you left out the part about the rose petals and silk." She smiled up at him.

"How about the fact that you still look eighteen years old?" His face came close to hers.

She couldn't resist tracing one of the well-shaped ears tucked against his head. "Did I ever tell you that you've got small ears for a Tennessee farmboy?"

"You mean they're supposed to stick out?"

"That's the stereotype, isn't it?" She sighed as his lips grazed the corner of her mouth. "We should do this more often."

"We should do this all the time." His voice rumbled through her bones. "Marnie, I want you to come to Rome with Cody and me."

She grew still. Hadn't she made it clear that she didn't want to be his playmate, but a real wife whose husband loved her with all his heart?

Yet she couldn't push him away. This time together was too precious to waste on quarreling.

He spoke again, into the silence. "I didn't mean I expect you to fly back with us right away. I know you've got a business to wind up. And with Granny's illness, this might not be the best time to leave. We could start making plans to get married again, though."

The mention of Jolene gave her an opening. "What about you?" She sat up and pulled the covers around her. "Don't you want to spend time here with Granny? Think how much fun Cody would have, playing games with her and exploring the farm."

A thin crease formed between his eyes. A worried look, she thought. "For her sake, I'd like to be here, but I couldn't do that to Cody, or to myself."

"Do what?" she asked. "You mean, put your career on hold? People in your field can take leaves of absence, can't they?"

She didn't just want him to stay temporarily. But she knew better than to push too hard, too quickly.

"It's not just a question of my career," he said slowly. "I love the Foreign Service, but I have to admit I'd like more flexibility as Cody grows up."

"There are more opportunities in Ryder's Crossing than you might think," she said.

"It's still a small town." Restlessly Tom threw back the bedspread and reached for his robe. "I want my son to grow up speaking several languages and feeling at home in different cultures."

"I admit, Ryder's Crossing is hardly Rome, but there's a Japanese community now, thanks to the new car manufacturing plant, and you'd be surprised how many people have moved here from Eastern Europe."

He shook his head. "A few immigrants can't change the small-town mind-set. I don't want my son getting hurt the way I was. He's different from the people here, and so am I, and I'm sure they'll find a thousand ways to make sure we don't forget it."

Without waiting for her response, he grabbed his shaving kit and went out. Marnie sank back against the pillow disappointed, and wondering if there were anything she could have said or done differently.

But she doubted it. Tom simply didn't want more children, and he wouldn't even consider living here. Cody might be adorable, but between Nonna Olivia and Tom, the boy was well cared for. He didn't really need Marnie and neither, she suspected, did Tom.

Maybe she should take a chance, anyway. It seemed less and less likely that she would ever love anyone else. Why not go to Rome and take what she could get?

Marnie pictured her store, the delight she took in choosing and displaying each item, the fun of story-time, the touching way older customers confided their loneliness to her as they selected gifts for distant relatives. She valued her work, and she knew she was helping ensure that as the town grew it never lost its heart.

Speaking of hearts, what about hers? It was capable of loving profoundly, but also of being profoundly hurt, as she'd learned. How could she risk everything a second time on a man whose feelings for her didn't run very deep?

Last night hadn't changed anything, Marnie reflected glumly as she put on her nightclothes and headed for her own room. The gulf between her and Tom remained too vast to bridge.

TOM DID HIS BEST to keep busy that morning. He took Cody to see Miss Lacy, whose low-slung belly nearly scraped the barn floor; he helped Granny figure out how to use the fax program in her computer; and he searched the attic for an entry hole, in vain.

It was probably lurking behind a couple of steamer trunks too heavy for him to move. He would have to wait until tomorrow when Mike would be there to help.

Tom's thoughts kept returning to Marnie. She hadn't refused his proposal, but she'd withdrawn emotionally. She still wanted him to come back here and be a traditional husband and father.

He loved her just the way she was; why couldn't she love him the same way? Why did she have to keep trying to turn him into something he wasn't?

By midmorning Tom was struggling to find things to occupy his time, especially since Cody remained absorbed in computer games. An aging house always needed work, so he oiled the door hinges and locks, but one day wasn't long enough for him to tackle any major projects.

After lunch he remembered the back staircase and found a key in a kitchen drawer. The flight, he discovered, was indeed steep and narrow, but it had been cleared of spider webs, so obviously Mrs. Wheedles knew about it.

All the exits were locked. No intruder could have accessed it, unless the cleaning lady herself were sneaking around in the middle of the night, which seemed highly unlikely.

He emerged on the lower level to find Marnie peering into the pantry, which was located near the staircase door. "Can you believe this?" she said. "We're having fried chicken tonight and there aren't any bread crumbs. Not even cornflakes or instant mashed potatoes."

It was news to Tom that one could make fried chicken with either of those substitutes. "Don't they make mixes in a bag?" he offered.

"You think Granny might buy one of those? You've got to be kidding!" She pushed aside a couple of items. "There isn't enough oil for deep frying, either."

"Deep frying might be bad for her heart, don't you think?"

"Of course it is, but she insists on it." Marnie threw up her hands. "She says life isn't worth living if she can't eat her favorite foods for Christmas. We need salad greens and tomatoes, too.''

''As I recall, the fresh vegetables at the Ryder's Mart were never very good.'' Tom loved the crisp Italian produce that Nonna Olivia selected each morning.

''Oh, there's a new supermarket. It's much better.'' She glanced toward the window. Outside, heavy clouds had begun moving in. ''I'd better make a grocery run before the snow hits.''

He didn't relish the idea of driving into town, but Tom *was* curious about her store. Besides, even though he'd been avoiding her all morning, he didn't want her to put any distance between them. ''I'll come, if that's all right.''

Marnie hesitated so long that he wondered if she were going to refuse. Then she said, ''Why not? I'll go tell Granny.''

Only as she walked off did Tom realize that, during the entire conversation, she'd never met his gaze, not once.

Chapter Nine

As they drove the five miles into town, the stark winter landscape played through Tom's heart like a bittersweet melody. Arriving here with Cody, he hadn't paid much attention to his surroundings, but now memories flooded in.

They crossed the creek where he used to go fishing, not for sport but because there was rarely enough to eat at home. It reminded him of being hungry, and ashamed of his poverty.

The houses they passed were modest, and several needed paint. Yet, to a boy who lived in a shack, they became palaces he would scarcely dare to enter.

Marnie took an indirect route so she could show him how the area was growing. Speaking like a tour guide, she pointed out a subdivision of homes so recently built they didn't even have lawns yet. Their raw unfamiliarity brought Tom back to the present.

Farther along, he saw a new section of Ryder's Crossing marked by a community hospital, specialty food shops and a pharmacy with signs in Japanese as well as English. Then they turned onto Ryder Avenue, the main street, and passed the high school.

The redbrick building loomed from his memory, monolithic and menacing in the gray winter light. Here Tom had arrived each day on the bus, bracing himself mentally for the battle ahead.

As the station wagon waited at a stop sign, he imagined he could hear the clang of lockers and smell sweat socks. His skin prickled at the memory of insults, some veiled, some open. Even worse had been the looks of pity as kids noticed his shabby clothes and badly cut hair.

But it was also in this building that he'd met Marnie. It was here that he'd first received an A on a term paper and an exam, and seen his teachers' faces reflect their astonishment and, eventually, respect.

It was in the school gymnasium that he'd taken out his frustration on the rings and the high bar, emerging at last from his self-absorbed fog to discover that he'd won the admiration of teammates. He'd also collected a couple of regional medals.

Tom straightened his shoulders. He wasn't that gawky, resentful boy any longer, he reflected with relief.

"Do you really hate Ryder's Crossing that much?" Marnie asked wistfully as she drove.

"What do you mean?"

"As soon as you saw the high school, your whole body language changed," she said. "It was like this other person, the guy you used to be, was trying to take over."

"Really?" It amazed him that she could see his reaction so clearly. "I didn't think it bothered me that much."

"You can unclench your fists now," she said.

Embarrassed, he relaxed his hands. "I know it's irrational, but for a long time after graduation I felt as if there was a vortex waiting to suck me into the past."

"That must have been awful." Marnie sighed. "Oh, would you mind if we stop by my store? I want to give Cody a book for Christmas."

"Sure. As a matter of fact, I was hoping to see your place."

Now that the wave of painful emotions had ebbed, Tom found himself enjoying the drive into the heart of town. The shops sported wreaths and strings of colored bulbs above frosted windows, and everything looked brighter.

The street was extrawide here, with room for angle parking spaces on either side. None of that tricky parallel parking, and not a parking meter in sight, he noted appreciatively. Of course, in Rome it was practically impossible to park anywhere. Like most residents, he used taxis, buses and the subway, or simply walked.

Some of the stores stood cheek-by-jowl along the sidewalk, but others sat back in freestanding buildings. Among the bland modern names beckoned a few eccentric ones: Ma Fremont's Durn Good Home Cookin' and What in Tarnation? Used Stuff You Don't Need.

The Italians, who loved pioneer themes, would enjoy this evidence of American originality, he reflected. The country's penchant for producing spaghetti Westerns had its roots back in Puccini's turn-of-the-century opera, *The Girl of the Golden West.*

Tennessee, of course, wasn't the Wild West of Annie Oakley and Wyatt Earp, but it had been a frontier in its day. Tom felt a stir of nostalgia whenever he heard a reference to Daniel Boone or Andrew Jackson, although, he had to admit, that didn't happen often in Rome.

They pulled into a parking slot beneath a sign that read, Afton Books, Stationery and Gifts. An array of children's books and cookbooks, set against cranberry and ivory drapes, filled the display window.

The use of Marnie's maiden name troubled Tom a little, although it made perfect sense. Everyone in town knew her that way, and of course she was single now.

"Aren't you coming in?" She paused with her door open.

"Sure." He swung out of the car into the snapping cold of the December air and the scent of cinnamon drifting from the Hickory Dickory Bakery next door. The beginning notes of "Jingle Bells" chimed as Marnie opened the door.

Following her, Tom found that the interior was larger than he'd expected, filled with an impressive number of books and racks of cards and shelves of stuffed animals and collectibles. The overall effect was eye-catching, but not cluttered.

A couple of browsers glanced up, and a familiar-looking woman in a red-checked dress hurried over. "My gosh! Tom Jakes! I can't believe it!" announced the slightly nasal voice of Marnie's best friend, Betty Simson.

It took Tom a moment to dredge up her married name, Wheeler. Her husband, Stewart, a quiet, self-effacing fellow, whose father owned a tailor shop, had been a fellow member of the gymnastics team.

She'd acquired some gray hairs and wrinkles, but her friendly expression hadn't changed. He'd almost forgotten that she'd stuck up for him once in an argument at school, and that Stewart had loaned him a tuxedo from his father's store when Tom couldn't afford to rent one for the prom.

Why hadn't he thought about them in all these years? he asked himself with a twinge of guilt. They deserved better than to have disappeared from his mind the moment he left Ryder's Crossing.

"How's it going?" Marnie asked.

"It's been busy," Betty chirped. "Wow! Tom Jakes!" She repeated his name as if he were some kind of celebrity. "We see your picture in the paper all the time!"

"Excuse me?"

"Oh, Robby's always running those wire-service photos of diplomatic conferences," she explained. "The ones with you in them."

Tom only appeared in news photos when he happened to be standing near a VIP. "I'm surprised the wire services would identify me."

"I don't know whether they do or not, but Robby puts your name in," she said. "We're so proud that someone from Ryder's Crossing does such important things!"

All he could say was, "Thank you." He supposed she must be exaggerating. Maybe one such photo had run; Jolene must have insisted on it.

He couldn't imagine that Robby Jones, as editor of the paper, would want to publicize anything positive about Tom. Surely the man who'd insulted him at graduation could only resent seeing a supposed inferior get ahead in the world.

"We just came in to pick out a book." Marnie took a deep breath. "For Tom's little boy."

Betty's face showed confusion, then surprise, then a twist of sympathy for her friend. Marnie had handled meeting Cody so smoothly that Tom had given little thought to how awkward this situation must be for her, since her best friend had to be aware that they'd divorced over the issue of not having children.

"I didn't know you were married," Betty told him. "Congratulations."

"I'm not." She seemed to be expecting some explanation, so Tom added, "Sometimes accidents work out for the best."

"Cody's the sweetest child," Marnie said. "I thought he might enjoy *If You Give a Mouse a Cookie*. Unless he already has that?"

"I don't think so." Tom selected most of his son's books himself. "I'm sure I haven't bought that one."

They made their way to the children's section. Surrounded by such a wealth of material, he couldn't resist buying a couple of extra selections for his son, including one about the life cycle of cats.

This store certainly reflected Marnie's personality, he thought as he waited in line to pay. It was well organized yet casual and colorful.

Until now, he hadn't fully appreciated how much of herself she'd invested here. It wasn't just time and money, but love that made the place so welcoming.

"As long as we're here, would you like to see my house?" Marnie asked when they were done.

He'd almost forgotten that she had a place of her own. Of course, he knew she didn't live on the farm anymore, but he hadn't been able to picture her anywhere else. "I'd like that."

She gave him a rueful grin. "Then quit heading for the front door. It's out the back."

Curious, he followed her through the store and the stockroom and out into a well-kept alleyway. The house on the other side had an unpretentious air and yet, as they circled it to approach from the front, Tom gauged that its solid two stories encompassed plenty of room for a family.

When Marnie ushered him inside, he inhaled the tang of pine oil and a hint of tomato sauce, no doubt left from preparing the lasagna on Wednesday. There was an airy openness to the living room and the dining room, which was beyond an arched doorway.

The completeness of the decor, from the patterned carpet to the antique-style chairs and tables, surprised him. It looked as if someone had spent a decade putting this place together. Then he remembered Jolene writing that the previous owners had sold the furnishings along with the house.

Outside, a few snowflakes had begun falling, and Marnie seemed anxious not to linger. Yet as she showed him through the modern kitchen and the rest of the downstairs, Tom wished he could spend some time here.

He'd like to watch her curl up in a chair so he could play the scene through his mind later, when he was back in Rome. He wondered which seat she preferred, and what book she was reading, and whether she carried her morning cup of coffee into the living room or drank it in the kitchen.

"I guess that's it," she said when they returned to the living room.

He indicated the stairs. "Is the second floor where you hide the stolen jewels? Or is it only off-limits to ex-husbands?"

For a fraction of a second she hesitated. "I didn't think you'd be interested."

"I am, if you don't mind."

Marnie shrugged. "No stolen jewels, I'm afraid, but you're welcome to see for yourself." She led the way up the stairs.

Her bedroom had a large four-poster but no canopy. Its classic decor featured a blond-oak dresser, a bronze freestanding halogen lamp and a sewing machine set on a small table.

Tom crossed to examine a crystal-framed montage of photographs above the table. There were her grandparents, serving cake at a child's birthday party, and her parents, riding horseback at the farm. There was Tom at college graduation, one arm around Marnie, their mortarboard hats nearly touching, their faces full of anticipation.

The shot that dominated the assemblage had been taken at their wedding, in the church where her uncle had officiated before moving to Chicago. Marnie, a garland of spring flowers in her hair, radiated joy, while Tom's broad smile reflected his sense of delight that this precious woman was marrying him.

Why did she keep these photos in her room, where she must see them every day? "Marnie?" he asked.

"Why didn't you toss these in the trash like any normal divorced woman?"

"Call me sentimental." The hoarseness in her voice undermined her attempt at flippancy, and she turned quickly away. "There are two other rooms up here, and then we should leave before the snow gets heavy."

"That might not be for hours." He didn't know why, but he felt an even stronger urge to hang around, now that he had reached her inner sanctum.

"Or it could turn into hailstones as big as cars!" she retorted.

"I take your point." Chuckling, he followed her across the hall.

The second bedroom was unremarkable, but the third one brought Tom up short: an oak crib took pride of place, flanked by a toy chest and a changing table. The pastel wallpaper sported frolicking kittens and puppies.

A lump formed in his throat. She must be expecting to meet Mr. Right and have his kids any day now.

"Aren't you getting a bit ahead of yourself?" He strove for a light tone.

"This belonged to the previous owners," Marnie explained. "I didn't see any point in redecorating until I decided what to do with the room."

He felt foolish. Naturally she'd no more purchased the crib than she had the sofa and hutches downstairs. Then he noticed a pair of oversize pandas cuddling atop the toy chest. "Did those come with it, too?"

"They didn't fit anywhere else." She tried to slip out of the room, but Tom was standing in the doorway, and he felt no inclination to let her by. "Seriously, we ought to be going."

"In a minute." He contemplated what might happen if he ran his hands along her arms, and decided not to press his luck. Not while she stood there bristling, as if prepared to defend her territory with tooth and claw. "Thanks for showing me your house."

"No big deal." Her voice caught.

"You've nested here," he said. "Settled in for the duration."

She let out a low cough. "It's no secret that I want a family, Tom."

"Met any likely prospects?" He didn't know why he pressed the issue, except that he wanted to hear what she would say.

"Well, there's Guthrie Phillips," she said. "You met him yesterday."

A jolt of alarm shot through Tom. "He's asked you to marry him?"

"He hasn't even asked me out on a date yet." She grinned. "But you seemed to expect an answer."

"'No' is a perfectly good answer," he said.

"So is 'Mind your own business,'" she retorted impishly. "Now if you'll just move..."

He stepped back, then changed his mind. At the same time, she started for the exit, and they bumped into each other in the doorway.

"Sorry," she said.

"I'm not." Cupping her face in his hand and stroking his thumb along her cheekbone, Tom leaned down to kiss her. He felt her tremble, but she didn't draw away.

The contact burned through him. Although they

touched only lightly, Tom throbbed with an awareness of Marnie in every inch of his being.

He slipped one arm around her waist and eased her closer. "We've got the place all to ourselves," he murmured.

She wavered, and then ducked into the hall. "No," she said, and skittered down the stairs like a frightened deer.

Well, darn. An old country boy like him shouldn't have let her get away. He must be losing his touch.

As Tom descended, he wondered why his suggestion had distressed her. They'd become lovers again last night, after all. "What's wrong?"

Moisture sparkled in Marnie's eyes as she turned at the bottom of the stairs. "This is my home. I'm saving it for—for the man I'll marry and have a family with."

Pain knifed through Tom, along with a scarlet flash of jealousy. He didn't want her to marry someone else and have children with that man. If only she could give him the unconditional love he needed!

Maybe he would never find a woman who could do that. Or maybe he would find her and discover that he couldn't love her back because he still loved Marnie.

Yet he knew he couldn't change her mind while they were in this house, with all that it represented to her.

"I guess you're right. Bad timing on my part." Releasing a long breath, he followed her through the front hall.

On the way past the living room, Tom couldn't help picturing Cody running into the room and squealing with delight at the sight of the bears. It must be something about the house, he told himself. Stick around long enough, and even a rover like himself might get domesticated.

But the temptation wouldn't last. A man never changed who he really was.

MARNIE SCOLDED HERSELF as she drove to the supermarket. What kind of idiot was she, showing Tom her house? Why hadn't she at least removed the wedding photos from her bedroom wall first, or thought about how he might react to the nursery?

The worst part was that she couldn't help noticing how naturally he fit into her home, filling up the empty spaces with his smooth, long-limbed movements. She'd left room for a man to add his own presence, and only now realized that the man in her subconscious had been Tom.

She couldn't see Guthrie Phillips there, or anyone else. Maybe, Marnie told herself fiercely, that was because most men would already own a house, or expect to choose a place together. It hadn't been very sensible to expect someone to adapt himself to her style.

Still, that couldn't account for the panic she'd felt when Tom suggested they make love in her bed. Was she afraid she'd never feel right bringing another man to her home after that? Or was she afraid of being left alone with a houseful of memories?

"Marnie?" Tom said. "If I went too far, I apologize."

"You didn't do anything wrong." *Except be the wrong man for me to fall in love with.*

"Is that why you're not meeting my eyes?"

"I'm driving!"

"Well, if you're not careful, you're going to wrench that steering wheel right off the post," he said.

She eased her grip, then promptly tightened it again and turned into the parking lot. It took all her attention to weave between the welter of shopping carts and bag-toting customers, and by the time Marnie parked, Tom appeared to have mercifully forgotten what they'd been discussing.

"This is a big store," he said as they got out. "I keep thinking of Ryder's Crossing as such a small town, but I don't recognize these people."

Marnie had had the same impression when she first returned here, that the town had grown so much she hardly recognized it. She missed the sense of knowing everyone and being known by them. Still, her bookstore depended on a growing clientele and, besides, it was useless to try to turn back the clock.

"The population's close to thirty thousand now, more than double what it was when we graduated." She pointed out license plates from Georgia, North Carolina and Kentucky. "Plus we get a lot of people passing through."

When they reached the sidewalk, Tom stopped at a coin-operated news rack. "Looks like the *Crossroads Journal* has expanded."

"It went from a biweekly to a daily half a dozen years ago." Marnie had still been living in Europe when that happened. "Since then, it expanded to a couple of sections a day, and four on Sundays."

"Does Granny subscribe?"

"No, I have it delivered to the store," she said. "I usually bring her the week's stack when I visit. Anyway, she gets most of her news from CNN."

Tom inserted some coins and removed the top copy. "This might be fun to flip through."

When they entered the store, he noticed cheerful, well-stocked sections for produce, seafood and flowers. From the on-site bakery wafted mouthwatering scents, and Marnie couldn't resist buying much more than bread crumbs and cooking oil.

"They'll be closed tomorrow," she noted. "Which do you think, blueberry pancakes for breakfast or apple?"

"Get both. Live dangerously." He wore a pensive expression that revealed nothing of what was going on inside. She wished she could read Tom's mind, but she'd never been good at that.

Maybe she should present him with her offer, after all. Was it possible he might consider it? Had this unplanned trip into town accomplished more than all the arguments she could have made?

Despite his insistence that he wanted to raise Cody abroad, Tom might be more ready than he believed to put the past behind him. By the time she'd paid at the cash register, Marnie was entertaining a guarded sense of hope.

They emerged from the store to find the snow falling more thickly and quite a few cars pulling in, perhaps prompted by concern about laying in supplies. Residents of outlying farms tended to maintain large winter stores of nonperishable goods and produced their own milk, but no one liked to run out of fresh fruit and vegetables. Or chips and other snack foods, either.

"Amazing," Tom said. "Where do they all come from?"

"You didn't believe me about how much the place has changed," Marnie teased.

He stashed their cart near the edge of the sidewalk and lifted out their two bags. "Sure, I did. But it's not the same as seeing for myself."

"Now that you have, there's something I want to discuss." She took a deep breath. "It's about the chamber of commerce."

But he wasn't listening. He stood frowning across the driveway at a family emerging from a minivan.

Marnie recognized the stocky, square-shouldered figure and her spirits sank. It was Luke Skerritt, president of the chamber and partner in the town's largest construction company.

Just when Tom was softening, why did his worst enemy from high school have to show up?

Chapter Ten

This, Tom decided, was ridiculous. He'd shaken hands with foreign ministers and gone out for drinks with two U.S. ambassadors, not to mention brainstorming over lunch with an undersecretary of state. Yet here he stood in front of a supermarket, tensing at the prospect of running into some kid he'd known in high school.

Well, not just some kid. Luke Skerritt had been class president for four years and captain of the football team.

He was also the son of the town's former mayor. They were the kind of people who wouldn't even hire Furnell Jakes to repair their basement, because they didn't want his kind hanging around their property.

And Tom didn't blame them. When his father needed money for liquor, he'd been known to swipe a few items.

Still, that didn't excuse the way Luke had treated Tom after he began excelling at school. Not only had he pointedly shunned Tom in the hallway, but his snide remarks about the gymnastics team had been seized on by some of the other students.

Then there was the rudeness of insulting Tom at graduation. He didn't suppose the man would be uncouth enough to make an unpleasant remark here in public, after so much time. But it was possible.

What Tom hated most, he admitted to himself, was that a part of him still cared. He didn't want to be vulnerable to a small-minded snob, but he could feel his hackles rising.

On the other hand, Luke looked different from how he'd looked in high school. Hadn't his shoulders been broader, or was that the pads in his football uniform? Tom certainly hadn't realized the man stood several inches shorter than himself.

Luke was helping a pretty blond woman, obviously pregnant, out of the van. Two boys of about five and eight waited politely for their parents.

It was typical of Luke to be wearing a suit, even on Christmas Eve at the supermarket. Always well dressed, always trying to outdo everyone else.

Tom couldn't suppress a rueful smile at his speculations. What was it that made this figure from the past loom so large in his memory? Luke probably didn't even remember him.

The Skerritts headed for the sidewalk. Tom's eyes met Luke's and he caught the shock of recognition.

Uh-oh. Testosterone time, he thought.

"Don't bite him," Marnie muttered.

"Do I look as if I might?"

"Bite him, chew him up and spit him out," she said.

"Me?" he asked in genuine surprise. "I'm not the five-hundred-pound gorilla around here."

"That's what you think."

He had to admit, the closer Luke got, the more changes he could see in the onetime football star. His face had filled out and his hair was streaked with premature gray. From his square build, it was clear Luke must be struggling to keep his weight in line.

But what had changed most was the man's expression. Not a hint of a sneer or a swagger; in fact, Tom could have sworn the man was a bit intimidated. Did he think Furnell Jakes's son would take a swing at him after all these years?

"I don't know if you remember me," Luke said as he ushered his family onto the sidewalk. "I'm Luke Skerritt, and this is my wife, Sue Anne."

Puzzled, Tom shook hands with them both. "Pleased to meet you, Sue Anne." Was Luke joking about not remembering him? Seeking a neutral remark, he added, "When's your baby due?"

"Two months." Mrs. Skerritt smiled up at her husband. "And this is positively the last one. It's a girl."

"Congratulations," Marnie said. "I hadn't heard."

Tom didn't recognize the woman, but he recalled Luke had attended Vanderbilt University in Nashville. Most likely they'd met there.

"We'll go on ahead," Sue Anne said pointedly, and steered her sons into the supermarket.

"So, have you—" Luke glanced from Tom and to Marnie and cleared his throat. "So have you visited the bookstore? It's fantastic, isn't it?"

"I was impressed."

"I trust your, er, Miss Afton has shown you some of the changes in our town," Luke went on.

Tom nodded. "You've been busy. At least, I presume your company has handled a lot of the building.''

''Our fair share.'' The man braced himself and folded his arms as if settling in for a chat. ''So far this town's been lucky. We've benefited from a trend toward industry moving to low-tax states like Tennessee, and people moving to more moderate climates. But we need to plan our growth for the future. Stimulate development and offer more to attract newcomers than mild weather and pretty scenery.''

He appeared to be in the mood for a serious discussion, although Tom couldn't imagine why Luke would care about his opinion. ''You mean entertainment? The arts?''

Luke cleared his throat. ''I don't think we can compete with the big cities in the South, let alone what you must be used to in Europe. But yes, that's the kind of thing I had in mind.''

''It would seem to me you'd want to assess what's unique about this area,'' Tom said. ''Its history and geology. Wildlife, crafts, anything that people can't readily find somewhere else. Build on your strengths.''

Luke regarded him thoughtfully. ''It seems so obvious when you say it, but believe me, those of us who've stayed here don't have that kind of perspective. We forget that there *is* anything unique about this area.''

Tom didn't suppose it would have occurred to him, either, until this trip. Now the dark, dignified silence of the pine forest, visible behind a nearby low-lying office park, awoke a sense of ancient things waiting to be lured into the open. ''I'm no naturalist, but I should think this could be an interesting area for a lot of activities.''

"I'd like to hear more of your ideas.'' Luke glanced toward the glass front of the supermarket. "However, Sue Anne has trouble lifting things into the cart these days, so I'd better get my act in gear. It's good to see you again.''

"You, too.'' Tom was surprised to find he meant it.

They shook hands again and the builder went inside, leaving Tom bemused. There had been a subtle shift of power, a hint that he was the one to whom Luke deferred instead of the other way around.

"He's mellowed a lot, hasn't he?'' Marnie nudged him into resuming their trek toward the car.

"I'll say.'' When she unlocked the back of the station wagon, Tom stowed the bags inside. "It sounds like he wants Ryder's Crossing to get even bigger, but then, what builder wouldn't?''

"You don't like the idea?'' Marnie asked.

"Consider me neutral on the subject,'' he responded. "I don't live here anymore, remember?''

She was headed for the driver's door, her face averted, and if she answered, Tom didn't hear her.

SNOW FLECKED THE windshield as Marnie drove, and patches of it were sticking to the ground. "I hope Uncle Norbert and Aunt Linda can get here from Nashville,'' she said. "Not to mention Cousin Mike. Heaven knows what time he's going to arrive.''

"They'll make it,'' Tom said.

A truck went by in the opposite direction, and it

was a moment before Marnie could make herself heard. "Why do you sound so certain?"

"Because it might be Granny's last Christmas," he said. "They'll find a way, if they have to do it on skis and snowshoes."

She half wished he hadn't reminded her. Her grandmother had seemed so normal lately that Marnie had almost forgotten the dire warning. Yet she did appear to have moments of weakness, and she did keep retreating to take naps. Her insistence on having Cody sleep in her room also implied a concern that there wasn't much time left.

"I can't imagine losing her," she said. "She's been my Rock of Gibraltar. When my parents died, if my grandparents hadn't been there, I don't know what I'd have done."

"Moved in with your aunt and uncle," Tom said.

"You make it sound so simple!"

He leaned closer to her, but perhaps it was only because his large frame needed more space. "Of course it isn't simple. But you're talking to a guy whose mother ran away when he was thirteen and whose father kicked him out three years later. I didn't even have an aunt and uncle to turn to."

"I know. It was awful." As a teenager, as much as she'd sympathized with Tom's plight, Marnie hadn't really been able to put herself in his shoes. No wonder he'd had such a bleak, edgy manner during his first few months at the farm.

"It was the best thing that ever happened to me," he said. "Remember what a lost soul I was? Mad at the world, and I hated myself worst of all. I'm not a fatalist, Marnie, but there's a part of me that believes things happen for a reason. Even the things that hurt us most.''

Did he include the breakup of their marriage? If she hadn't left, he wouldn't have Cody, so Marnie supposed a great good had certainly come from the pain. But that wasn't much comfort to her.

''I don't believe everything happens for a reason,'' she said. ''But I do think we have a choice about how we react to things. We can usually find some positive path to take, if we look hard enough.''

What would hers be? she wondered. To marry Guthrie or some other man, who could never set her blood on fire the way Tom did?

She thrust up her chin, determined to be positive. Just when things looked darkest, a glimmer of hope usually appeared, and she would find it.

When they got home, she was disappointed to see that none of her other relatives had arrived yet. Doc Spindler had stopped by, though, and was teaching Cody how to play Go Fish. Although the little boy couldn't keep his cards straight, he enjoyed shouting ''Go fish!'' at the top of his lungs.

Marnie baked bread from dough Jolene had let rise earlier. She was setting it on the counter to cool when she noticed that Tom, seated at the table with a half-empty coffee cup in front of him, had become absorbed in the newspaper.

Since taking his father's position as managing editor, Robby Jones had introduced a livelier, fresher style. He'd managed to do it without dropping traditional features like the almanac, so he'd kept old readers while winning new ones.

None of which explained why Tom was staring at

an inside page as if it were the most fascinating thing he'd ever come across. In fact, she calculated he'd reread the same item a couple of times.

"What *is* this?" he said, finally.

"What is what?" When he didn't respond, Marnie said, "I can't see through the page. What are you reading?"

Tom glanced at the heading. "Criss Crossings. That's Robby's column, apparently."

"His version of town gossip," Marnie agreed. "He's got a good ear for what's going on around here."

"Is he known for his sarcasm?" Tom frowned at the page.

"Sarcasm?" Robby sometimes wrote scathing editorials about state legislators, but he never directed the sharp side of his pen against local residents. "Not particularly."

"Well, he mentions a few distinguished visitors in town for the holidays, and he put my name in there," Tom said.

"So?"

"What do you mean, 'so?'"

"Why shouldn't he?" Marnie asked. "You are a distinguished visitor."

"To Robby Jones?" Tom quirked an eyebrow. "The man who called me a fraud and said someday he was going to expose me?"

"I think he's gotten over his delusion about your cribbing your term papers." Marnie smiled at the notion. "Tom, that was years ago! It's perfectly obvious I'm not helping run the U.S. Embassy in Rome for you!"

His blue eyes took on a reflective distance. "That's right, Betty did mention him using my photograph." Abruptly, he rattled the paper. "Yes, but a few paragraphs below he mentions that the chamber of commerce is searching for a director. He's italicized the qualities they're seeking. Let's see… 'a sophisticated sensibility' and 'the awareness to expand our horizons.'"

Marnie got a sinking feeling. "Yes?"

"Here's the kicker," Tom went on. "It says, 'Could we persuade one of our distinguished visitors to look homeward again?' You're involved in the chamber, Marnie. What's this about?"

She couldn't duck the issue any longer. "They want to hire you as the director. I'm supposed to offer you the job."

Sheer astonishment animated his face, but he mastered it quickly. "Why haven't you?"

"Because I'm a coward," Marnie said. "Anyway, I knew you wouldn't take it."

"You're darn right!" he flared. "What a crazy idea!"

She might as well press on. "On the other hand, they're promising a decent salary, with benefits."

"Sounds thrilling," he muttered.

She barely resisted the impulse to scrunch up a paper towel and fling it at him. "This town's turning into a city. One of these days we're going to need a real mayor, not a part-time figurehead, and you'd be first in line for the job."

"Me?" He grimaced. "Tom Jakes, mayor of Ryder's Crossing?"

She couldn't tell whether he was belittling the prospect, or stunned at the turnaround in the way he was being regarded. "I wish you'd at least think about it."

He folded the newspaper, his expression troubled. "All right," he said quietly. "I will."

Setting the paper aside, he rose and walked out of the kitchen. A moment later Marnie heard the front door close behind him.

She wanted to call him back and demand he share his thoughts with her. But it was in Tom's nature to keep his deepest feelings to himself. As she'd done so many times before, she had to let him go and simply hope he would come back.

IN JOLENE'S ROOM Marnie found Cody curled up asleep on the bed. Her grandmother and the doctor sat on opposite sides of the Scrabble board, glaring at each other.

"I've never seen anyone take so long to make a play!" complained Artie when he looked at Marnie. "Next time, I swear I'm going to time her!"

"You're just upset because you're losing," Granny said. "Look at that, Marnie. I got a triple-word play *and* a triple-letter on Z. Now, how many points is that?"

"Too many!" Artie dumped the tiles into the box lid. "You win. No need to trumpet how badly you've trounced me!"

The doctor appeared to be mostly bluffing, because he gazed at Jolene with affection when she wasn't looking. She, in turn, insisted on escorting him to the front hall, despite Marnie's concerns.

"I don't want you overtiring yourself," she told her grandmother.

Dr. Spindler frowned. "She needs to move around, Marnie. Keep the circulation going."

Silently she resolved to buttonhole him right after the holiday. Jolene had never been willing to discuss her heart condition in any detail, let alone see a specialist. Maybe Artie wasn't supposed to break doctor-patient confidentiality, but if her grandmother weren't receiving all the help she needed, he had no right to keep Marnie in the dark.

Now wasn't the time for confrontations, however, so she remained behind. The bustle as the older folks departed must have awakened Cody. Just after they left the room, his eyelids fluttered and he stretched.

"*Ciao*, Marnie." He gave her an angelic smile. "Where's Daddy?"

"He went out for a little while." She hesitated, torn between wanting to spend time with the little boy and trying to protect herself from getting too attached.

"Can I see Miss Lacy?" He bounced to his feet.

"Sure." Swallowing the lump in her throat, Marnie reached for his hand. "Let's go."

Outside, the snowfall had slowed. The placid farm-yard scene, the crispness of the light and the dance of flakes through the still air made her feel as if she'd been transported inside a glass paperweight.

They waved to Jolene and the doctor, who stood near the carport. Tom's rental car, she noticed, was missing.

When they got closer, she realized the older couple were arguing over whether to consider *byte* a legal word. Apparently it wasn't in the old dictionary they'd been using.

"What about *Internet?*" Jolene demanded, continuing the debate. "I suppose you wouldn't have allowed that one, either!"

"You can use computer jargon if I can use medical terminology!" Artie responded. "Otherwise, if it isn't in the dictionary, it doesn't count!"

It was a good thing, Marnie reflected as she escorted Cody to the barn, that among her wrapped gifts lay a new dictionary for her grandmother. It would obviously come in handy.

Inside the barn the air was warmer by a few degrees. "Where's cat?" Cody asked.

"She has to be around here somewhere." Miss Lacy rarely deigned to answer to her name, but Marnie called out, anyway, and heard a faint mewling from the tack room.

She knew at once what had happened. It occurred to her that it might be difficult for Cody to leave once he'd seen the kittens, but it was too late; he'd broken free of her and was running toward the tack room.

Marnie hurried after him. Although she knew her grandmother didn't store dangerous chemicals or sharp implements carelessly, Cody was too young to wander around alone.

Close behind him, she entered the small room. It took a moment for her eyes to adjust.

Although she thought of this as the tack room, there was no horse-related equipment left in the dimly lit space, only wooden workbenches, pegboards on the walls and a tall cabinet at one side. Beneath a bench lay an old wooden box stuffed with rags, and there lay a ginger-striped ball of fur, watchfully reclining among her new brood.

The kittens, their eyes still shut, were half hidden beneath their mother. Cody stopped a few feet away as the cat got to its feet.

"Gattini!" The little boy peered at them in delight. "Kittens!"

"Don't get any closer," Marnie advised. "They're too little to play with."

She thought she counted five, but she couldn't be sure. In any case, she was more interested in watching Cody's reaction.

With his soft blond hair, lighter than Tom's, he made an appealing picture as he crouched there. She circled to see his chubby face, dominated by blue eyes that tilted slightly, like his father's. It gave him an elfin appearance, as if he were an old soul tucked into a new body.

Miss Lacy relaxed, reassured that her visitors meant no harm. A low rumble echoed through the room.

"Listen!" Cody beamed at Marnie. "Happy noise!"

"She's purring."

He tried to brrrr with his lips. "I can purr, too!"

He ought to spend more time on a farm, she thought. But Cody was hardly deprived simply because he lived in a city.

On the other hand, he *was* deprived of a mother. Nonna Olivia had children and probably grandchildren of her own. Besides, if Tom were reassigned, it was unlikely the housekeeper could move with him.

A child shouldn't be shuttled from caretaker to

caretaker, Marnie thought. Especially not when his single dad had to spend so much time at work.

The boy needed a mother. With a rush of longing, she acknowledged how much she needed a child to hold in her arms and keep. Maybe it didn't have to be some as-yet-unconceived baby. Why not this special little boy?

Cody belonged to Tom, and he'd made it plain that Ryder's Crossing would never be their home. She must not allow herself to fall in love with a child who could never be hers.

"I want the spotted one." Cody pointed at the kittens.

Marnie followed his gaze. "That's what people call a calico." A black patch over one ear gave the little creature a rakish air.

"We take it to Rome?" He regarded her expectantly.

"Oh, no!" Marnie realized he was too young to understand about the realities of living with a father in the Foreign Service, so she explained, "He's too young. He needs his mommy."

"I want him!" Cody's mouth set stubbornly.

"Do you get everything you want?" she responded, and realized she sounded just like her mother, long ago.

"No," the little boy admitted, and made a helpless gesture with his hands. "I love kitty."

"Of course you do," she said. "He's cute, isn't he?"

Marnie had witnessed enough temper tantrums in her bookstore to realize how strong-willed children could be, yet Cody had backed down without a fuss.

She understood now what Tom meant about his son having an easygoing temperament.

Yet it didn't seem right to take advantage of the child's good nature. Just because he didn't insist on getting his way, that didn't make it right to ignore his feelings.

"I'll tell you what," she said. "In a few months, when the kittens are big enough, I'll adopt two of them. The spotted one for you, and another one for me. They can play together while I'm at work."

"Can I see them?" he asked.

"Whenever you and your daddy visit Granny," she promised. "Maybe someday you can take the calico cat to live with you."

It was possible that Tom might eventually be stationed in Washington, D.C., she told herself. She would keep her pets indoors, so Cody's cat would feel at home in an apartment. "Now, how about a little snack, and then..."

Outside, a car pulled into the driveway. With a rush of anticipation, Marnie went to see if it was Tom, but she didn't recognize the dark blue sedan resting where Dr. Spindler's vehicle had been a short time ago.

She recognized the middle-aged couple inside, however, the gray-haired man very straight and dignified, the woman smiling warmly at her grandmother. As the doors opened, Marnie launched herself forward. "Uncle Norbert! Aunt Linda!"

The next few minutes blurred into a series of hugs, introductions to Cody and exclamations of delight. Although her aunt and uncle were reserved by nature, they'd been pillars of Marnie's life as long as she could remember, and she loved them.

After her parents died, she knew her aunt and uncle would have liked a daughter. However, they'd graciously accepted her grandparents' insistence on raising Marnie themselves, letting her know they would always be available if she needed them.

Uncle Norbert had officiated at her wedding, even though he must have had doubts about Tom's family. It had been a relief when Furnell Jakes declined to show up. Her aunt and uncle had seemed genuinely pleased about Tom himself. They'd never made a negative comment about her divorce, either.

Now Norbert studied his mother-in-law with concern. "Are you sure you're well enough to be outside?"

Jolene, who had been hugging Linda within an inch of her life, wilted beneath his gaze. "Oh, I rest every chance I get. I'm just thrilled you finally made it."

Linda gazed hopefully around. "Has Mike arrived yet?"

"He called two hours ago," Jolene said. "He should be here soon. Perfect timing, eh?"

"It would seem that way." Norbert's guarded manner might appear cold, but Marnie suspected he was as eager as his wife to see their son.

The last time Mike had seen his parents, bitter words had been exchanged, followed by months of silence. Now he was coming to the homestead for Christmas. Marnie could feel the tension as her aunt and uncle prepared to see their prodigal son.

In the meantime she carried one of their suitcases into the house, and her uncle took the other. Cody scampered ahead to the upstairs den where they would be sleeping. It lay directly across from Marnie's room and next to Tom's.

She'd been wondering whether she and Tom would have another night together, but now she realized how unlikely that was. Marnie would never be indiscreet around her old-fashioned aunt and uncle.

By the time the suitcases were stowed and everyone reassembled downstairs, it was almost time to start frying the chicken. As Marnie tied on an apron, however, she heard the rattle of an old vehicle in the driveway.

That wasn't Tom's rental. It had to be Mike.

She followed her grandmother, Cody and her aunt and uncle out the front door. Sure enough, a rusted van was dieseling to a halt near the other cars.

Through the driver's window, a shaggy-haired man waved at them. In the past few years, Marnie's cousin had grown thinner, and his skin had lost its youthful smoothness, but there was no mistaking that playful gleam in his eye.

Linda started forward, then halted as someone emerged from the passenger side of the van. From behind the others, Marnie glimpsed a young woman with olive skin. She wore a loose smock and her hair in two thick, black braids.

"Oh, dear," Norbert muttered under his breath. "He's brought some hippie."

"Hi, everyone!" Mike hopped out of the van, and Marnie saw he was wearing torn jeans and a tie-dyed T-shirt, à la sixties. She wondered if he'd selected the outfit on purpose to annoy his parents. She certainly hoped he hadn't selected his girlfriend that way.

''Hello, you scamp!'' Jolene reached him first, with a big hug. ''This must be Bonita!''

With a sinking feeling, Marnie realized her grandmother had done it again. As much a rascal as her grandson, she'd withheld information from the rest of them.

''Did you tell them?'' Mike demanded.

''Tell us what?'' Norbert regarded his son through narrowed eyes.

''I wanted you to give them the good news yourself!'' Without letting him get a word in edgewise, Jolene added, ''Linda, Norbert, I'd like you to meet your new daughter-in-law. And look who else!''

There was more? Marnie wondered dazedly, and then she saw that Bonita had just unstrapped a baby from the backseat of the van.

Chapter Eleven

When he left the house, Tom had no idea where he was going. He simply got in the car and drove.

He needed to sort out his impressions. To integrate what he'd seen and experienced that day.

The word *mayor* kept careening around in his head. It was foolish, crazy, self-defeating even to consider it, he told himself. Marnie had simply mentioned that such a prospect might exist.

Until today Tom would have dismissed such speculation as outside the realm of possibility. Maybe it still was. But he understood now that Marnie's conjecture was based on more than her own blind faith in him.

Betty's admiration had been his first clue. Still, Marnie's friend had always treated him courteously. She was a natural cheerleader who made those around her feel good about themselves.

That didn't explain Luke Skerritt's reaction to Tom. He hadn't feigned his respect. He'd actually seemed pleased that Tom remembered him.

As for Robby Jones, the newspaper editor had put his views in print for everyone to read. Although he hadn't named names, it was obvious he wanted Tom to head the chamber of commerce. Who else among the "distinguished visitors" fit the "sophisticated sensibility" requirement? The others, as Tom recalled, had been a fly-fishing champion and a retired mathematician.

He had to admit, some of his objections to Ryder's Crossing no longer held up. He'd been afraid of subjecting Cody to small-town snobbery, but there appeared little danger of that. If people valued the father, they would treat the son decently, as well.

As the town continued to expand, it would indeed require strong, caring leadership. However, he noted grimly, it also needed and deserved a man who could make a lifetime commitment to it, and that wasn't the future Tom saw for himself.

He liked the man that he'd become, and the career he'd built. He might be a small player on an immense stage, but he relished the sense that he was making a difference in the world.

One town could never be enough. In high school, Tom had dreamed of getting away, but later he'd realized that he didn't simply want to escape to another place. He needed travel, new cultures and the freedom to keep moving.

He'd found a job that offered him that. He'd be crazy even to consider giving it up.

The snow had stopped, although the sky remained a moody gray that promised more to come. Absorbed in his thoughts, Tom didn't pay much attention to his surroundings until he spotted a familiar dirt road ahead, nearly overgrown as it cut through a field of wild grasses.

A wall of emotion hit him like a tsunami. It took all Tom's presence of mind to slow the car, turn off the road and stop.

He hadn't wanted to come here. He'd only been back once in sixteen years, to collect his father's few, worn possessions and to find the will scrawled on a ragged sheet of paper.

"I don't want no grave. Give my stuff to my son and tell him I'm sorry." That was it, his father's last testament.

From the unkempt state of the road and, beyond it, the tangled woods, it was obvious no one lived here now. Tom wasn't even sure who owned this land; maybe some large corporation or the state. He vaguely recalled his father doing some work for an absentee owner once, but no doubt the property had been sold since then.

He felt repulsed at the prospect of visiting the place where he'd grown up. The shack where his mother had spent so many miserable years before fleeing. The house where his father had thrown him out in a drunken rage when Tom was sixteen.

Still, he'd instinctively driven here. Might as well take a look around; he refused to let a few grim memories spook him.

Tom never allowed himself to yield to fear. Giving in meant giving up.

Once, while making preliminary arrangements for an undersecretary of state's visit to a former Communist country, he'd been warned that as an American official he might become a target of zealots. Each time Tom screened a hotel site or dropped by a government office, he'd been aware of how little protection his two armed escorts could really provide. But the mission was important, so he'd shoved his fears aside and taken care of business.

What faced him now wasn't physical danger, of course, but long-buried emotions. The threat was that they might shake his equilibrium and pull him away from Marnie just when they were becoming close again.

With a mental shrug, Tom swung his car onto the bumpy lane. Deep ruts reminded him of how nearly impassable the road became in rainy weather. The winter cold, however, had firmed the soil, and the rental easily navigated the distance across the field and into a clump of pines.

Cones littered the ground and crunched beneath the tires as Tom put the car into Park and switched off the engine. A chill silence fell.

The house, never much to look at, was now little more than a pile of lumber with a caved-in roof, and the bricks had crumbled around the well in the front yard. At the edge of the woods, the refuse heap had decomposed until its origins were indiscernible.

Exiting the car slowly, Tom inhaled the scent of rotting pine needles. There had been worse smells, in the old days.

It was not the kind of place to which a boy would have brought his friends. He'd shown it to Marnie once after his father died, and had been humiliated by her look of shocked pity.

What would his sophisticated friends in Rome think if they saw where he'd grown up? Would they guess that in moments of self-doubt he considered himself a fraud?

Tom got out and slammed the door, startling several birds into flight. The refuse pile rustled, and a squirrel whisked across his line of sight.

Burrs and weeds snatched at the cuffs of his pants as he walked toward the house, and an invisible miasma thickened around him.

Tom didn't feel like the articulate man that others saw. He felt like the boy from the back of nowhere, with holes in his shoes and loneliness in his gut.

It hadn't always been so terrible, he reminded himself with a mental shake. When Mom was here, sometimes she would ask how his day had gone, and cook spaghetti for dinner. She had made curtains from thrift-shop castoffs, and when she hung laundry from the trees, it billowed like sails on a magic ship.

He tried to summon an image of her, and slowly it came: blond hair, blue eyes, a thin, worn face and a tired smile. There weren't any photographs; his father destroyed them when she left.

Tom stepped through a gap where the front door had been. The house was even smaller than he remembered.

There was a modest front room, an alcove where his mother had cooked on a camp stove, and, in back, a narrow add-on for his parents' bed. At the sight of the rotting couch to his right, Tom's ribs throbbed with the memory of sleeping on broken springs.

The place smelled like mold. Come to think of it, it always had; in the past he'd simply taken it for granted. Rains swept often across middle Tennessee, keeping it green in more ways than one.

Lord, this was a miserable place, Tom thought. It was hard to imagine living here. Only hurricane lamps to study by, a rickety table and hardly any books. Even his mother's Bible got moldy.

Any decent person, observing his family, would have experienced sympathy. At the time he'd expected only scorn. In any case he didn't remember anybody ever coming here.

He opened a rickety cupboard. The mismatched dishes were still there, a few chipped cups bearing a rose pattern that his mother loved. After his parents' fights would come a lull when Furnell begged her forgiveness and gave her little gifts that he scavenged. Tom wasn't sure where his father had found these cups.

Now that he reflected on it, the quiet times must have been much longer than the explosions, but in retrospect they lacked the impact. His father hadn't always been so violent, either. When Tom was little, Furnell had worked more frequently and they'd eaten better. There'd even been new clothes for Easter once.

As his father's drinking increased, though, meanness seemed to boil out of him more. Tom had read that some people suffered a predisposition to alcoholism, but he didn't consider that an excuse. The man must have seen how he was hurting his family.

Tom didn't want to be bitter. He'd been lucky to find Marnie and her grandmother. He'd clawed his way out of this mess and, happily, hadn't inherited a weakness for alcohol.

But he recognized that he possessed a dark side of his own. He could feel it as he stepped from the shack and heard his father's harsh voice call, "Get back in here, boy!"

Instantly Tom's hands formed fists, and his back

stiffened. When he'd let loose against his father in self-defense, he'd been stunned by his own rage. He'd sworn never to unleash it against anyone else, and he never had.

This anger was what powered him to run risks and seek new challenges. He had channeled it into a constructive path, but it festered within him, restless and unresolved.

Whenever he thought of coming back to this town and trying to live like a tame creature, he could feel the savagery welling. He would never raise a hand against anyone he loved, but he might yell things he didn't mean, and words could hurt as much as blows.

Tom didn't want to find out if it were true. He had no right to ask Marnie to trust him and then risk destroying her happiness.

He'd tried to explain all this to her once, but she didn't believe him. She maintained a blind faith in the redemptive power of love. Well, Tom's mother had once loved his father, and it hadn't saved either of them.

Yet that didn't mean he and Marnie couldn't find a way to be together. If only she loved him enough to accept the way he was, to come to Italy with him, to be satisfied with the child he already had. Not to ask more of him than he could give.

At the thought of Marnie, Tom's tension vanished. He warmed to the image of her quirky, mischievous smile and the remembered softness of her in his arms. Why was he wasting time wallowing in the past, when he could be sharing Christmas Eve with the woman he loved?

Suddenly he couldn't wait to get home.

WHEN HE REACHED THE FARM, Tom witnessed a curious tableau. Marnie and her aunt and uncle stood as if frozen, staring at a group of people near a rundown van.

The objects of their attention were a baby, its dark-haired mother and a young man in need of a haircut. Tom had once known Marnie's cousin Mike fairly well, but he wouldn't have recognized the man today if they'd passed each other on the street.

The only moving figures were Jolene, who was stroking the baby's cheek, and Cody, who jumped up and down excitedly beside Marnie.

It didn't take a genius to get the picture. Mike had sprung a surprise wife—at least, Tom hoped they were married—and child on his parents. The nearly empty homestead had suddenly become crowded, just when Tom would prefer that everyone disappear.

He wanted to talk to Marnie alone. It might take every bit of diplomacy he'd acquired, but he meant to persuade her to come away with him.

Mission deferred. With a sigh he got out of the car and went to say hello.

His arrival, however, snagged only perfunctory notice except from Cody, who ran to tell his father the kittens had been born. Norbert, Linda and the newcomers, after a moment of shocked silence, were all trying to talk at once.

Norbert asked, "Who is this?"

Linda added, "You have a baby?"

Mike responded, "I figured Granny would mention it."

The dark-haired woman said, "You didn't tell your parents? You didn't tell them *anything?*"

Beneath his shaggy brown hair, Mike blushed. "I, uh, figured they'd find out soon enough."

"But you promised to tell them!" The woman tossed her black hair, then stepped toward Linda. "Hello, I'm Bonita. Mike and I got married four months ago, a month before Josefina was born. He said he invited you to the wedding, but I can see he did not."

It didn't take a genius to get the picture, Tom reflected as he hoisted Cody onto his shoulder. Mike must have feared his parents would disapprove of a bride eight months pregnant. And Mike had never liked taking the consequences of his own actions, even if it only involved facing his parents' displeasure.

Now his cowardice had left everyone else to struggle with an awkward situation. Linda handled it graciously, as usual.

Her mild face reflecting genuine welcome, she said, "We're delighted to have you in the family." She reached for the baby, which Bonita surrendered after only a split second of hesitation. "What a darling! My first grandchild!"

Norbert shook hands with his daughter-in-law. "I'm glad we're meeting you, even if we did miss the ceremony. Are you from Santa Fe?"

"Yes, for three generations."

Introductions were made, and Tom greeted this new family member with admiration. She obviously had a lot more pride and backbone than her husband.

Mike appeared somewhat abashed. He was likely to receive a tongue-lashing later, Tom thought, and he richly deserved it.

They went inside, this knot of people who to him seemed like dozens. There was no way to get Marnie alone now, he saw as she and her aunt Linda went to start dinner, so he commandeered Cody to help him set the table.

He would have to bide his time. But he didn't intend to leave Ryder's Crossing without Marnie's promise to come to Rome.

THE KITCHEN BUSTLED with activity. Marnie fried the chicken, Linda was baking rolls, and Jolene sat at the table to fix the salad.

Bonita joined them, shooing the menfolk away so she could breastfeed. Little Josie, with her crop of black hair, was so cute Marnie could scarcely take her eyes off her.

Watching the baby, she wanted one of her own so badly she could taste it. Although she'd begun bonding with Cody, it obviously hadn't displaced her deep maternal craving for an infant.

Marnie wanted to hold a sweet baby against her and know that it belonged to her. That she was the mommy to whom her little one would turn with its hurts and joys.

She longed to watch over her newborn as it grew— one day at a time. How did the miracle happen, that such a helpless creature began to walk and say words and develop a sense of humor?

Dear as he was, Cody was already a personality in his own right, and she would never try to erase his love for the other women who had helped to shape him, Elise and Nonna Olivia. Yet a primitive, instinctual part of her also longed for a child who could be entirely hers.

And Tom's. With a pang she acknowledged that he was her husband still, in her soul. She wanted a child with him. Would he ever want one with her?

It was impossible to brood, however, with so much conversation ping-ponging around her. Linda was full of questions, and Bonita cheerfully answered them.

Her family owned the music store where Mike worked. She was the youngest of four children and, until she'd fallen in love, had planned a career as a singer.

Bonita also had questions for Jolene about the farm and for Linda about her home in Chicago. Once the baby finished nursing, she snuggled into Jolene's arms, and Bonita insisted on carrying platters of food into the dining room. Linda beamed at her daughter-in-law.

Norbert said grace, and dinner was accompanied by lively conversation. Mike, however, who sat at the foot of the table wearing a hangdog expression, did not participate. He looked so pitiful, Marnie had trouble restraining her laughter.

As she buttered a roll, she sneaked a glance across the table at Tom. He'd changed into a powder-blue sweater that gave his eyes an electric brightness.

With his calm, poised manner, he looked every inch a man of the world. Yet she knew him well enough to sense that his mind had been in turmoil this afternoon when he left.

Where had he gone? Had he reached some kind of resolution?

She'd seen, this afternoon, how surprised he was

at the reaction he'd received from the townspeople. Especially Luke and Robby.

Since she returned to Ryder's Crossing four years ago, Marnie had gotten to know them as adults and nearly forgotten how cocky they'd been in high school. Surely Tom could see how they'd changed.

She hoped he would realize how much this town needed him. Yet she nearly burst with pride when she saw his picture in the newspaper or heard from Granny about some conference at which Tom had assisted.

Was it asking too much for him to give it up? Was she being selfish?

After dinner the men washed dishes and then everyone gathered in the living room. Outside, the wind was picking up, and the weather forecast called for heavy snow. Inside, warm and cozy before the fire, Marnie played the piano and they all sang carols.

Bonita's rich voice impressed her, although her new cousin never tried to show off. She didn't need to. It was a joy to listen to her velvety tone.

Mike watched his wife with a rapt adoration Marnie had never expected to see on his face. She wished Tom would gaze at her that way, but he wore a distant expression.

Was he remembering Christmases past, perhaps during high school, or their Yule in Stockholm? She wished, not for the first time, that she could read his mind.

Cody and Jolene both began yawning at the same time, and Norbert admitted to being tired from the flight. When he and Linda retired upstairs, Mike took

Josie and Bonita to the downstairs sewing room, where they were to sleep.

His parents had offered to switch, since the den was larger, but Bonita preferred being close to the kitchen. A nursing mom got hungry at night, she said.

She still hadn't forgiven her husband for keeping his parents in the dark, though. Every time Mike peeked at her hopefully, Bonita's chin came up and she focused on someone else. Marnie figured their room's isolation at the back of the house, providing privacy for what was sure to be a heated conversation, was one of the reasons Bonita preferred it.

Cody vanished into Jolene's room, where he'd slept soundly last night. Best to keep him there again, Jolene informed Tom in a tone that brooked no argument, and he didn't give her one.

It was fine with Marnie, too. As soon as the house got quiet, she intended to gather her courage and slip into her ex-husband's room.

She hoped that today he'd realized that he belonged here with her. Or maybe, she thought with a twinge of apprehension, he was going to break her heart.

Chapter Twelve

In the bedroom Marnie debated whether to change into her nightclothes, but decided against it. Visiting her ex-husband's bedroom at night wasn't something her uncle would approve of if he spotted her; she didn't want to compound the problem by making it obvious they'd become lovers again.

Besides, she wasn't sure she wanted to resume their involvement of the previous night. What she needed was to talk.

Forcing herself to wait until Norbert and Linda were likely to be asleep, she tried to read a murder mystery, but the words refused to connect in her mind. Finally she gave up.

Oh, heck, she didn't need to skulk here like a guilty adolescent. She was a divorced woman in her thirties, and if she wanted to meet a man at night, that was her business.

Marnie swung out of bed and was astonished to find her knees going weak. Why on earth was she so nervous?

Because whatever Tom says tonight, it matters. More than anything.

A tap at the door sent her heart leaping into her throat. It was a moment before she could answer. "Yes?"

The knob turned and Tom peered inside. "May I come in?"

"Of course." Quickly Marnie ushered him in and shut the door. "I was just going to sneak down to your room."

He grinned. "Do you feel about sixteen? I do. Except we never did anything like this when we were sixteen."

"I should say we didn't!" As a teenager, Marnie had fallen asleep many nights imagining Tom kissing and holding her, but she'd never allowed her imagination to stray beyond that. For them to have been able to go on living in the same household, they'd both known they had to remain platonic friends.

It was different now. She heard his quickening breath, and her blood heated in response.

Nevertheless Marnie was determined not to let nature take its course. At least not yet, so she sat at her dressing table. "Where did you go today?"

There were no other chairs, so Tom sat on the bed. "To Dad's house, or what's left of it."

"Was it difficult?"

"Yes."

He didn't elaborate, and she decided not to pry. "Have you given any more thought to the chamber of commerce job?"

His lowered eyelids gave him a hooded expression, like a hawk. "Naturally."

"I don't want to pressure you or anything." Hearing her own words, Marnie knew that wasn't true. "Oh, yes, I do! Take the job!"

He chuckled. "Your enthusiasm is flattering."

His easy manner reassured her, although Marnie knew his moods could be mercurial. "For once, Tom, let other people's opinions influence you. You're respected around here. Admired. And wanted."

"Just by people in general?" he teased.

The half-dozen feet between them stretched like a football field. It was much too great a distance across which to carry on such an intimate conversation.

Marnie scooted across the floor to him. It gave her an odd sensation to be sitting beside Tom on this bed where she had slept for her first eighteen years. And yet it felt exactly right.

He reached for her, and she sought shelter against him, secure in his strength. She tilted her face up to his, and their mouths joined in a passionate kiss.

She wanted him to take all of her, even those bits and pieces that she had held in reserve for years without being aware of it. And she wanted him to share everything about himself.

"I love you," she murmured.

"Oh, yes." Tom's voice was ragged, as if he felt pain and pleasure at the same time. "Marnie, my wife."

Muscular arms drew her onto his lap. One hand ruffled her hair, lifting it from her neck, while his tongue slipped into her mouth.

Sensations poured through her, blending and burning. She inhaled his tantalizing male scent and reveled in the controlled power of his lips against hers. Possessively his hand eased her blouse from her waist-band.

Beneath her, she felt Tom come to life. Only a few thin layers of cloth separated his male arousal from her core.

Groaning, he shifted her onto the sheets. As his kisses trailed down her throat toward her erect nipples, Marnie gasped in delight.

Then she remembered her aunt and uncle across the hall. "We'd better do this quietly," she whispered.

He lifted his head. "That won't be easy.... Darn!"

"What?"

"I forgot the protection." His mouth quirked in self-reproach. "We'll have to go to my room."

She had never made love to Tom without some form of birth control, Marnie realized. Maybe that was why she'd always sensed a barrier between them.

"I don't want you halfway," she blurted. "I want everything."

His grip on her slackened. "Marnie, you know I don't want children."

It was a terrible time to press the issue. Her common sense told her to go with him, to make love without risking pregnancy, to save her arguments for another day.

But what other day would there be? "I don't want you to leave without—" Did she dare explain that she loved him so much she didn't want anything to come between them, even if he left her afterward? "Just this once."

Sitting so close, she could tell that Tom remained ready for her. His heartbeat hadn't slowed, and he must be as eager as she was to touch and rub with no clothing in the way.

But his mood had changed. He was retreating into the part of himself where she could never enter. "Is that it, Marnie? You want a baby more than you want me?"

His statement shocked her. "How could you think that?"

"It's what you said."

If she hadn't been so stunned, she would have weighed her words more carefully. But his accusation stung, and without thinking she made one of her own. "You did it with Elise!"

Stiffly, he got to his feet. "So that's what this is about."

"No!"

"I thought I made it clear that was an accident," Tom said. "I won't be so foolish again."

Foolish. The air vanished from Marnie's lungs as if she'd been struck.

She hadn't even been thinking about a baby tonight. Her emotion was more elemental than that, a longing to be joined with Tom in every sense.

Why did he insist on holding her at arm's length? Denying her, even once, the true intimacy he'd shared with a stranger?

"One time—" A parched throat made her cough, leaving the sentence unfinished. *One time isn't likely to make me pregnant.*

"It isn't just one time." His low voice bristled with anger. "You know I couldn't abandon my own child. I'd be trapped here forever."

"Trapped?" Was that how he felt, not only about Ryder's Crossing but about staying with her?

"I'm sorry." He ran his fingers through his hair, mussing it. "I know you're not trying to trick me, Marnie. You're being up front about this. But I can't do it."

"I don't want a child as much as I want you."

"Then come to Rome with me."

"I can't." Her tone sounded plaintive, even to Marnie. "Not while you insist on keeping me at a distance. Not while you won't give me what I want most."

"I thought I was what you wanted most." He watched her like a wild creature, tempted toward domesticity but afraid of the trap.

"I want all of you."

"I see."

She didn't think he did, really, but she couldn't find the words to explain it. They were friends at a deeper level than she had ever experienced with anyone else, and yet he didn't love her fully, the way a husband loved his wife. Holding nothing back.

It wasn't exactly about having a child. Yet the distinction was so fine, she wondered if she were fooling herself.

Tom released a long breath and met her gaze with rueful irony. "So that's that. I guess I'd better sneak back to my room before the grown-ups catch us."

Marnie hugged herself against the evening chill. "I guess so."

He lifted a corner of the quilt and tucked it around her. "You look cold." His jaw worked, as if he wanted to say more or even kiss her again, but he just walked away. The door shut quietly behind him.

She should have tried to explain better, Marnie thought glumly, yet every time she voiced her viewpoint, it got filtered through Tom's tangled mental processes and twisted out of shape. How could two articulate people misunderstand each other so completely?

MARNIE DREAMED of reindeer clattering on the roof and Santa sliding down the chimney with his bag of toys. "Ho, ho, ho!" he cried in a high-pitched voice, and landed with a thump.

She awoke abruptly. The noise of Santa's arrival reverberated in her brain, but the room was bathed in silence.

Despite the gray morning light, she wished she could doze off again. She'd tossed and turned until well past midnight, replaying the scene with Tom and trying to figure out what she could have or should have said, until she conceded that nothing would have made any difference.

The barrier between them wasn't a simple misunderstanding. It grew from their different natures and needs.

Across the hall a board creaked. Someone had decided to get up, and no wonder. Christmas morning was always a special time at the farm, and more so this year than ever.

The whole family had come home, bringing two new and very precious little ones. If this were truly Granny's last holiday, they ought to treasure every moment of their time together.

With mingled anticipation and reluctance, Marnie got out of bed. She could hear her aunt's and uncle's voices in the hallway, but not the deep rumble of Tom's voice.

Before she faced the world she wanted one private glimpse of last night's snowfall. At the window she drew back the curtains and blinked against the dazzle.

Against the rosy transparency of dawn, the landscape gleamed like a bride in her gown. A white veil swathed the earth, hiding the ruts in the driveway and the barrenness of the fields. Long gloves transformed the limbs of the naked trees, while the pines stood proudly beneath their temporary cloaks.

The scene filled Marnie with a sharp sense of longing for things that couldn't last. Maybe she ought to go to Rome with Tom, after all. Maybe she ought to content herself with half a loaf, if she couldn't have the whole thing.

Otherwise she might find herself looking back at this Christmas day, this wonderful moment that would never come again. The holiday when it snowed right on cue and when the people she loved were gathered around her.

Overhead the ceiling jolted. A series of bumps shook the room, and then, thinly but clearly, she heard a dry voice announce, "Ho, ho, ho!" Followed by giggles.

What was going on in the attic?

Pulling on her robe and slippers, Marnie went into the hall. Norbert and Linda paused halfway up to the attic, and she saw Mike coming from below with his wife and baby Josie.

"Somebody's sure making a racket up there."

Mike yawned and barely remembered to cover his mouth in time.

"Is this some kind of tradition?" Bonita asked.

Marnie shook her head. "It's a mystery to me. We've heard noises in the attic the past few nights, but nobody was shouting 'Ho, ho, ho.'"

She didn't think Cody's "angel" could be connected to this playful Santa Claus. Come to think of it, that dry voice had sounded a lot like Granny, but it was just plain crazy for a woman with a heart condition to be scampering up three stories and shouting the family awake.

Marnie had half a mind to go call Dr. Spindler, until she spotted him on the stairs behind Bonita. "What are you doing here?"

His eyes twinkled. "Your grandmother invited me."

"I didn't hear the doorbell."

"She gave me a key, ages ago." He smiled. "I worry about her living alone, so I look in from time to time. She can't always answer the door right away."

It didn't take a genius to put the clues together. Artie and Jolene were obviously much more of an item than Marnie had realized.

When he reached the second-floor, Marnie started to introduce the doctor to Bonita. They were interrupted by more shouting from the attic. "I said, 'Ho, ho, ho!' Where are you slug-a-beds?"

"I guess we'd better get up there." Artie winked. "We wouldn't want Jolene to give herself stitches."

"Stitches?" Marnie reproved. "Aren't you worried about her heart?"

"Well, sure." The old doctor tickled Josie's little bare toe, which stuck out from her blanket. "If we don't get up there, we're going to break it for her!"

The baby cooed. Bonita smiled and, accepting her husband's outstretched hand, continued their ascent.

Marnie let the doctor go ahead of her, which he did with zest. Torn between wanting to investigate her grandmother's shenanigans and wondering where Tom was, she lingered a moment on the landing.

And then he came down the hall, pulling a green V-neck sweater over his white shirt and tan slacks. With his hair brushed and his face damp from washing, he looked remarkably presentable compared to the rest of the family.

"This isn't a diplomatic emergency," she told him. "You didn't have to get dressed."

"You never can tell," he joked, and stopped a few feet away. "Marnie, I...I don't remember exactly what I said last night, but I should have— I mean, what I meant to—"

"You, too?" When she drew a puzzled look from him, Marnie said, "I was absolutely brilliant the tenth time I replayed our conversation. That must have been around midnight."

A slow grin animated his face. "My eloquence would have astounded you. But I think it took me until at least one."

She was tempted to ask if he'd changed his mind about anything. But Tom wore a wary expression she recognized from his teenage years.

It was the look of a wolf that's come in from the storm but isn't sure it belongs in a civilized world.

Besides, with laughter drifting from upstairs, this was no time for a heart-to-heart.

He touched her elbow. Suppressing a quiver of response, Marnie let him take her arm, and marched alongside him to the attic.

At the top of the stairs the modern chandelier spilled light across the space. Observing how its etched glass panels swayed in a draft, she could see how they might turn into prisms when the light came from the right angle.

To her left, in the open area, the knot of relatives had gathered. Peering between them, Marnie saw Granny garbed in pink tulle, with painted cardboard wings sprouting from her thin shoulders and a wire halo tilted rakishly atop her white hair.

"That costume's from the church's Christmas pageant!" Marnie told Tom. "What on earth?"

"I think we've identified Cody's angel." He chuckled. "Although I can't imagine how she managed to sneak around without being detected."

Hearing his name, Cody popped out from behind Jolene. He wore striped pajamas and an oversize Santa Claus hat that drooped down over his ears.

"*Buon Natale!*" He pitched himself toward his father.

Tom scooped his son into his arms. "Merry Christmas to you, too!"

"Come closer!" called Granny. "What's wrong with you people? Don't you want your gifts?"

The others were regarding her with varying degrees of amusement. Mike stared with obvious curiosity at the open trunk beside her, which overflowed with gifts wrapped in shiny metallic paper.

"Since when do angels bring presents up to the attic?" he asked.

"I'm helping out. Santa wore himself to a frazzle last night and he's sleeping it off!" Granny crowed. "Do you people want your goodies, or are we going to stand here debating the fine points of Christmas etiquette?"

"Wait a minute." Marnie felt she and Tom deserved an explanation. "Did you sneak up here a couple of nights ago? Did you lure Cody up here? What's going on, Jolene?"

The use of her given name must have jolted her conscience, or at least alerted her that she was in trouble. Sometimes, Marnie felt like the elder of the two, or at least the more responsible one.

With a hint of bashfulness, Jolene said, "I do apologize. Folks, I played a little joke on my granddaughter and Tom. But how else could I persuade them to let Cody sleep downstairs with me? He's such a cute little tyke, I wanted to keep him for myself a few nights."

The explanation didn't ring true. Why had she really wanted her great-grandson downstairs? Marnie didn't like the suspicion that crept over her, but she could hardly ignore it.

Granny had schemed to leave her and Tom alone together on the second floor. To drag them out of bed in the middle of the night and throw them into each other's company. And possibly each other's arms.

The worst part was, it had worked. But the long-term result was likely to be a disappointment.

"I don't understand how you pulled it off," Tom said. "We came right upstairs when we heard the noise. How did you sneak away without getting caught?''

Granny gestured toward the back of the attic. ''I took the servants' staircase. It's steep, but heck, I need my exercise, don't I, Artie?''

''I don't understand.'' Bonita, who had surrendered the baby to Linda, regarded her new relatives with a mystified expression. ''Mike said you were very ill. How can you run around like this?''

''Good question,'' Tom muttered.

''Did I say I was ill?'' Granny asked.

''Yes,'' growled Norbert, and a chorus of voices seconded him.

''Is she?'' Mike asked Artie. ''You're her doctor.''

''He's the doctor?'' Bonita looked even more confused.

''She does have a heart condition,'' he said.

Although she'd been well aware of that fact, Marnie couldn't suppress a touch of sadness at hearing it confirmed.

''You see?'' said Granny. ''Now—''

''It's called having a heart as big as all outdoors,'' Artie continued, running his fingers through his thinning hair. ''Aside from that, this woman is as healthy as a horse. You can take that as an official diagnosis.''

Relief rushed through Marnie, followed by annoyance. Thank goodness her grandmother was all right, but how dare she put her family through an emotional wringer?

The others were obviously thinking the same thing, and a roomful of accusing faces turned toward Jolene. ''You caused us all this worry for nothing?'' demanded Linda. ''Mom, that was wrong.''

"Well, how else was I going to get you stubborn people together?" she demanded. "Just imagine, a son who won't even invite his parents to his wedding! And a man who's afraid to tell the woman he loves about—well, about a lot of things!"

Emotions warred in Tom's expression. He fought them down, except for the redness that tinged his cheeks.

"You said this might be your last Christmas." Norbert wasn't going to let his mother-in-law off the hook that easily. "Do you know how concerned we were?"

Granny clasped her hands together and tried to look contrite, but she couldn't pull it off, so finally she gave up. "Well, I might get hit by a truck," she said. "Who knows?"

Bonita gasped. "What an attitude!"

"Granny doesn't mean it," Mike said. "She's just trying to escape the consequences of her own actions. You were my role model, you know, Granny."

That brought Jolene up short. "Excuse me?"

"You got away with being mischievous. In fact, people thought it was funny," said her grandson. "And you used to cover for me, remember? Like that time I ate half the cake and left a huge mess on the table."

"That was you?" Linda said. "Mom, you said it was the cat!"

"We didn't have a cat," Jolene reproved, as if that were an excuse.

"I thought you must have gotten one!" her daughter snapped. "Animals are always showing up around here! No wonder Mike was incorrigible!"

Norbert slipped an arm around his wife's waist.

"We can't entirely blame Mother Jolene," he said. "We indulged the boy ourselves."

Mike bristled. "No, you didn't! I used to get blistering lectures from you!"

"Lectures, but no follow-through on the punishment," his father admitted. "I should have talked less and acted more. Thank goodness you've come out all right in the end."

"On that note," said Granny, "Cody, would you help me hand out these gifts?"

She'd weaseled out of taking her medicine yet again, Marnie noted. She didn't exactly approve, but her grandmother's high spirits were infectious, and she had to admire her gumption.

Soon the attic filled with the sound of rustling paper as packages large and small were delivered all around. Jolene clapped her hands sharply, halting the process of unwrapping.

"What are you doing?" she cried. "I meant for you to carry these downstairs and put them under the Christmas tree! With the other gifts!"

"You mean we can't open them?" Mike asked in dismay.

"Not until after breakfast," Granny chided. "Good heavens, where are your manners?" She regarded the lot of them as if they were spoiled children. "And let's not hear one bit of griping about cholesterol and saturated fat, shall we? I want my sausage and eggs, and I want them now!"

"I absolutely insist on pancakes," Tom said above the din. "Or waffles. I'm not picky."

"What about preserves?" demanded Linda.

"Mom, you've got a whole pantry full of them from last summer. No hogging them!"

"Personally, I could use some coffee," said Norbert.

They trooped downstairs, laughing. On the way, Jolene adjusted her tilting halo several times before finally taking it off. "I guess it knows I'm a fraud," she said.

Tom caught Marnie's hand as they left the attic. With so many people around, there was no chance to speak, but he made it clear he held no animosity from last night.

Marnie was glad. She refused to think about the fact that he and Cody would be leaving tomorrow for their home halfway around the world. Today she wanted a truce.

Thank goodness Granny's health was fine, but for Marnie and Tom this really might be their last Christmas together. She intended to savor every moment.

Chapter Thirteen

It took the better part of an hour to get breakfast on the table, even though—or perhaps, because—all of them were participating.

Tom was surprised to discover how much he enjoyed the bustle. Unlike Bonita, he hadn't grown up in a big family, and although he'd spent Christmases at the Afton farm before, he didn't recall it ever being quite so busy and exciting.

In part, he recognized, it was because he couldn't help seeing events through the eyes of his son. Cody was in heaven, darting from room to room, fingering the shiny gifts that he itched to open, inhaling the wonderful cooking scents and hugging everyone who crossed his path.

For Tom, something inside felt fundamentally different. It was his rare sense of contentment, he supposed, but there was more to it than that.

Linda noticed, too. "You don't seem as fidgety as you used to."

"Fidgety?" As a man of the world, Tom hardly thought such an adjective applied to him.

Marnie's aunt regarded him with an air of maternal

solicitude. In the past, he'd assumed that motherliness was just part of Linda's character, but now it occurred to him that her concern was specifically for him.

Somehow, over the years, she'd come to care about him, as if he were part of the family. Was this new, or had he simply never realized it before?

The truth was, he reflected, that he'd been so prickly, he hadn't been willing to accept the concern of others. The role of outsider felt so comfortable, it was hard to relinquish it. Or had been, until now.

"I used to get the feeling that you'd rather be anywhere else than Ryder's Crossing," she said as she arranged bowls of cranberry sauce, applesauce and stewed fruit on the dining room sideboard. "But not today."

"Why on earth would I want to be anywhere else?" he said. "What better place could there be on Christmas than Granny's farm?"

"I don't know." Linda smiled. "I certainly can't think of anywhere."

After she left the room, Tom finished arranging the red candles in a ceramic candelabra, as Jolene had requested, and located matches in a drawer. He touched a match to the first wick, then the others and watched flames leap up.

The scent of pine drifted from the living room, where Bonita was telling Cody a story while she nursed the baby. From the kitchen came friendly conversation and the sizzle of sausages.

Home, he reflected. This was home.

Had he always yearned, until now, to be somewhere else? Tom supposed he had. Even during those last years in high school when he'd been grateful to take shelter here, he hadn't felt that he belonged.

He'd been searching for a long time without realizing it. For a place that was entirely his.

Tom set the candelabra in the center of the long dining table, which was laid with the Danish stoneware that Marnie had sent her grandmother from Copenhagen. They'd purchased the teak-handled bronze flatware on a trip to Thailand.

Over the years, he realized, this place had become invested with bits and pieces of his life with Marnie. Memories leaped at him—the little shop in London where they'd bought that silver platter; the gallery in Washington in which they'd found the Grandma Moses reproduction on the wall.

Every item had been exclaimed over and lovingly purchased and sent or brought back to the Afton farm. Why should he want to be somewhere else? Everything and everyone that mattered was here.

Cody ran in, proclaiming that he needed to eat right this instant. As if on cue, Artie appeared with a plate of waffles, followed by a parade of family members bearing one mouthwatering dish after another.

In her midcalf denim dress, with red and green smocking on the yoke, Marnie was the very picture of a modern country woman. Her modesty couldn't disguise her alluring femininity, and her obvious vitality only added to her appeal.

They gathered at the table and joined hands, and Norbert said a prayer. A low vibration seemed to run from one person to the next, linking them.

For the next half hour there was little time for chatter as everyone loaded up plates and surrendered to delicious indulgence. Tom was glad for the silence, because, for once, talk could only be superfluous.

He gazed around at the faces, young and old, familiar and newly met. At Mike, glowing with love for his wife; at Linda, sneaking glances at her granddaughter in the portable crib; at a beaming Artie and slightly smug Jolene and good-natured Bonita and thoughtful Norbert.

He tried not to linger too long on Marnie, although it was hard to pull his eyes from her soft brown hair and sweet face. Tom caught her glancing at him once, but she looked away quickly.

Cody insisted on sitting next to Marnie, and she left her own food to cool while she cut up his waffles and sausage. As she retied the oversize napkin around his neck, the two of them leaned so close together that their heads touched, and she brushed a kiss across the little boy's cheek.

Tom's heart squeezed.

He had never expected to feel such conflict at the very moment when he was happier than he'd been since Marnie left him. He didn't want to give this up, this sense of family, of belonging.

Yet he had to. Not only did his career lie elsewhere, but he knew his restlessness would return. It wouldn't always be Christmas; no holiday lasted forever, even in one's heart.

He couldn't commit himself to staying in the town from which he'd fled more than a dozen years ago. And he couldn't build a life with a woman, no matter how dear to him, who didn't love him completely.

Marnie did care for him; he had to admit that. Perhaps he had been unfair last night to accuse her of wanting a child more than she wanted him.

What troubled Tom was that she didn't want him *without* a baby. He needed to know that he was enough all by himself.

A marriage could crumble so easily. It had already happened to them once.

Much as he ached to have Marnie back, Tom had to be sure that she would stay no matter what. Losing her twice might be more than he could bear.

He had to make her understand. He would find the chance today, and this time he wouldn't waste it on futile arguments.

After they ate, people carried their dishes to the kitchen, scraped and stacked the plates and put the leftover food away. They gathered beneath the twinkling lights of the Christmas tree to open their gifts.

"One at a time!" Jolene announced. "That's the tradition. Besides, we're all hopeless snoops. We want to see what everybody else is getting."

"Any candy must be shared," Artie added. "Unless it's mine."

"I'm afraid we didn't know you would be here," Linda apologized. "Or Bonita, either."

"Oh, I got extra stuff." Jolene waved away the concern. "For Josie, too."

Tom volunteered to distribute gifts with Cody's eager help. Soon the carpet was piled with glittery wrappings and fancy bows. People were exclaiming over handcrafted items Jolene had bought at country boutiques, books and games from Marnie's store, Italian leather wallets and purses that Tom had brought in plentiful supply, anticipating extra guests.

Marnie held up the rose-colored sweater he'd packaged with her new purse, and he was pleased to see that it brought out her warm coloring. But her main gift would be given later, in private.

She'd obviously had trouble deciding what books to pick for him and had solved the problem by giving him a selection. There was one by Paul Theroux, his favorite travel writer, along with a historical thriller set in Italy, a humorous phrase book and an analysis of the possible future effects of the Internet on foreign relations.

"These ought to keep me busy for a while," he teased. "Thank you."

The books weren't a very personal gift, he thought, but then, she hadn't seen him in years. He supposed she must have been nervous about this encounter. He'd spent a few sleepless nights, himself.

Mostly Tom had wondered how she would react to Cody. No need to worry on that point. She was leafing through a new picture book, reading phrases aloud, to the child's obvious delight.

Jolene, who had slipped out of the room to shed her angel costume, returned garbed in her gifts. A Mexican-style skirt from Santa Fe swept the floor with its ruffle. It was topped by a reversible embroidered housecoat that Norbert and Linda had purchased. Tom's embossed leather pocketbook was tossed over one shoulder.

"Everyone ready for the fashion show?" she demanded, and circled the room like a model. A sparkle at her throat drew Tom's eye to a delicate necklace that must have come from Artie.

"Splendid!" cried the doctor, leading the applause.

"Best of all..." Returning to her favorite chair, Jolene dug beneath some wrappings and came up with the thick, new dictionary from Marnie. "I'm going to study this thing and trump your scrawny rear end at Scrabble!"

"Did I forget to mention that I'm giving one to Dr. Spindler, too?" Marnie asked. "I didn't realize he'd be here this morning, but please come by the shop next week, Doc. I'll wrap it, if you like."

"No need," he chortled. "We'll see who has the better memory around here!"

"It's a matter of strategy, anyway," Jolene said with a sniff. "Some people rush things, and they end up making mistakes. I know how to bide my time."

"You can say that again. I've never seen you make a move in less than ten minutes," Artie said with a twinkle.

Even Norbert had relaxed. "Mother Jolene, I may not always approve of your methods, but I want to thank you for bringing us together with our son and daughter-in-law."

Bonita poked her husband, who cleared his throat, saying, "That reminds me. I have a few apologies to make."

To his credit, his father refrained from saying it was about time. He merely folded his hands and waited.

"I've put my parents through a lot of grief," Mike said. "It was unfair to my wife, too. I can't change the past, but I *can* promise that in the future I'm going to face up to my responsibilities. I don't want to lose what I have, and I don't intend to."

Linda sprang across the room, hugged her son and

burst into tears. Tom noticed Artie wiping his eyes, and even Marnie sniffled a couple of times.

"As you say, what's done is done and can't be changed," Norbert said. "We forgive you for your shortcomings as we hope you'll forgive us, and we look forward to many happy times together."

"We would like you to visit us soon," Bonita added. "My parents want to meet you both!"

In the midst of the general conversation that followed, Granny suddenly flung wide her arms and cried, "What's that?"

Everyone stilled. From upstairs came a faint but unmistakable scratching noise.

"What *is* that?" asked Marnie.

They trooped into the hall, to the foot of the stairs. "Could it be from the attic?" Linda asked.

"Too far up," said Artie.

Tom knew better. "The acoustics in this house would surprise you. Sound funnels right down the stairs."

"I nominate you to go up and check on it," said Mike. "I'll be right behind you. About ten feet behind."

"What was that about turning over a new leaf?" It was the first time Tom could recall hearing Norbert tease anyone.

"Okay," his son said with a sigh. "Five feet behind." Tom led the way, moving stealthily. Trailing him, Mike kept quiet, too.

The scratching resumed, then stopped, and he heard the click of toenails on the wooden floor. A moment later he stepped into an attic filled with sunlight.

Near the back right corner crouched their little burglar, its eyes ringed with black, its bushy tail quivering. Not such a little burglar, now that he got a better look. It was almost as large as an Irish setter, but rounder and fluffier.

Mike let out a low whistle. "I didn't know raccoons grew that big."

"They do, indeed," said Tom. "They're pretty cheeky, too."

The critter assessed them as if debating whether to fight or flee. Then, not rushing, it turned away and ducked under the edge of the rafters.

"Where's it going?" Forgetting his fears, Mike raced past Tom. "Can't we catch it?"

"I'd rather not, thank you." Tom had a healthy respect for denizens of the wild. "It's on its way outside by now, anyway. I'd recommend we find the hole and seal it, and cut back whatever tree it's using to climb up here."

Soon the two of them were fetching building materials and a saw. Tom didn't mind being put to work. It provided an excuse to get out of washing the dishes.

"SO YOU WEREN'T our only nocturnal intruder," Marnie, scrubbing the last of the large pots, told her grandmother.

"I'm sure glad I didn't run across that tough customer while I was creeping around." Now that she admitted to being healthy, Jolene had been universally elected to do some of the dirty work, and was towel drying with gusto. "I'd have suffered a heart attack for sure!"

Based on Mike's description, the raccoon must be nearly as big as a cow, but Marnie figured her cousin was exaggerating, as usual. "In that angel getup, you'd probably have scared him out of his wits."

"I never heard of a coon keeling over from surprise," her grandmother returned tartly. "I'm not even sure they have wits. Are we done here? Artie's waiting to play Scrabble."

It was as good a time as any to ask the question foremost in Marnie's mind. "So, are you going to marry that man?"

"And spoil a perfect relationship?" Granny asked incredulously.

"Has he asked you?"

"I beg your pardon!" Jolene said. "I think that's my business."

"Don't risk losing him," Marnie warned. "You can't tell me you enjoy being alone here."

"Well, he *hasn't* asked me," her grandmother said. "The man's perfectly happy with the way things are. And so am I!"

"You don't sound very happy," Marnie murmured.

Her grandmother shot her a quelling gaze. "Speaking of being unhappy, let's talk about you and Tom."

"Let's not." Marnie had no intention of discussing her situation with her grandmother. Last night's encounter had been too intensely personal to put her feelings into words. "'Fess up, Jolene. You've brought the horse to water but you can't make him drink."

The animal analogy tickled Granny enough that she confessed, "He complains about how long I take at Scrabble, but I've been waiting for his proposal since who-knows-when. The man's entirely too comfortable, if you ask me."

"Then make him uncomfortable," Marnie said.

She caught a wink from her grandmother. "Not a bad idea." Reaching back, Jolene untied the apron from around her neck.

"Since we're finished, I think I'll take Cody to see the kittens." Marnie dried her hands. "He's been bugging me all morning."

"Coward!" Jolene snapped her towel into midair. "You're avoiding Tom, aren't you? Grab that man while he's in the vicinity, girl, or you'll live to regret it."

"I could say the same to you!"

"A man who's ducking a commitment doesn't deserve to be grabbed!" Jolene replied. "Even if he does have a cute rear end. Don't you think so?"

"Dr. Spindler? I can't say that I've ever noticed." With a sigh at her grandmother's irreverence, Marnie took off her apron and went to find the little boy.

The house was stuffed with people. Everywhere she turned, she saw her family enjoying their gifts, playing with the baby and examining each other's photographs.

She kept expecting to run into Tom, but he was still in the attic with Mike. In a way it was a relief.

But she saw him, anyway, in her mind: tousled and warm last night; freshly washed and dressed in the hallway this morning; studying her through the candles at breakfast.

She still had no answer to his invitation to come to Rome with him. How could she commit herself to a man who cared for her more as a friend than as a true husband?

Without him, Ryder's Crossing would be empty. But if they were married, a part of her would forever remain unsatisfied.

Why did life have to be so complicated?

Marnie found Cody in Jolene's room, playing a computer game with Artie. Observing the screen, she saw that the game involved little round men beating up dinosaurs.

"Isn't that too violent for children?" she asked.

The doctor looked up guiltily. "Do you think so?"

"Who picked this game, anyway?"

Artie swallowed. "I don't remember."

"He did!" said Cody.

"Me?" Artie surveyed the room as if some invisible guilty party might appear.

The little boy laughed and clapped his hands. His shining face reminded Marnie of Tom, but she valued this child for himself, not for who he resembled. "Want to go see the kittens?"

"Yes!" He jumped to his feet, nearly tripping over the doctor's feet in his hurry.

Artie didn't object. He leaned forward, snatched the controller and began madly bashing dinosaurs.

It took a while to get the child into his warm coat and hat, but Marnie insisted on taking every precaution even though they were only going to the barn. Cody was very young, and could easily catch a chill.

They walked outside together, mittened hand in gloved one. The breeze stung Marnie's cheeks, but she loved the freshness of the air and the scent of the forest.

The gently rolling landscape of middle Tennessee lacked the drama of the Smoky Mountains to the east, but she found beauty in its quiet splendor. Sprawling woodlands still covered much of the land, where pioneers had come centuries earlier, when this was the American frontier.

Through the bare trees deer were visible, grazing a short distance away. Marnie estimated the snowfall at four or five inches with deeper drifts, but some of the pines sheltered patches of bare grass that provided forage.

Pulling his hand free, Cody scampered ahead to the barn. As Marnie followed, her breath plumed around her face.

The barn was warmer, and, in the tack room, Miss Lacy lay across her brood like a fur coat.

"Where is Clico?"

It took her a moment to register that the boy had condensed the word *calico* into a name. "Somewhere under there."

He crouched close to the wooden box but made no move to disturb the kittens. Their mother watched him cautiously.

"There!" Cody pointed. "I see him!"

Marnie glimpsed a black patch against tan and white. "That's him, all right. Or it could be a her."

"My kitten!" said the child, his blue eyes brilliant with excitement.

He sat on the wooden floor and resumed watching the kittens, although they lay scarcely moving. They held his interest far longer than Marnie would have expected.

The creak of floorboards announced that someone

had entered the barn. She recognized the footsteps, balanced and firm.

"So." Tom eased into the tack room. His fleece-lined suede jacket and matching cap made him resemble a frontiersman, but there was nothing hard about his face. "What's all this?"

"That's Clico!" Cody showed him the kitten. "He's mine."

One eyebrow lifted. "Yours?"

"I'm going to take him home with me when he's older," Marnie explained. "Cody can visit him anytime. Or take him to live with you whenever you like."

Tom's mouth opened as if to address her, then turned instead toward his son. "You know, we won't be coming to Tennessee very often."

"Yes!" Cody glared with as much force as a two-year-old could muster. "Often!"

"I don't know what the quarantine regulations are regarding taking a cat to Italy," Marnie ventured, "but maybe..."

Tom shook his head. "It wouldn't be fair to the cat. He'd have to stay indoors all the time and be moved from place to place and sometimes left in a kennel. Cats need to roam and establish their own territory."

"So do children." The words escaped before Marnie had time to think about them.

"Oh?" Tom tilted his head. "What do you mean by that?"

She didn't want to discuss personal matters in front of the child, but he appeared absorbed in the kittens.

"How can you leave all this behind? Cody's so happy here."

"You haven't seen him in other places," Tom reminded her. "He adjusts easily wherever we go."

"Maybe on the surface...."

"I think I know my son...."

They hovered on the edge of a quarrel. Both stopped.

Regret twisted inside Marnie. "It's useless, isn't it?"

"No," Tom said.

"We can't agree on anything!"

"Maybe we just need to try harder." He loomed over her, strong and gentle, and she ached to press her cheek against his jacket. To be sheltered by him and not have to worry anymore.

If only she didn't need more than he could give. More, perhaps, than he was capable of giving—not due to any deficiency in himself, but to his distorted childhood.

Yet she refused to accept that he was incapable of moving forward. Just as, long ago, she had seen through the rebellious boy to the sensitive spirit inside, she now knew she perceived more in Tom than he recognized in himself.

She had to find a way past his guard, but so far everything she tried seemed to backfire. Or perhaps she was a victim of her own wishful thinking.

"Marnie, we need to talk privately," he said.

She sighed. "Now? Here?"

"Listen!" Cody jumped to his feet. "Santa's coming!"

"Sweetie, Santa already went back to the North

Pole. Remember what Granny said—'' Marnie stopped as a noise thrust itself into her consciousness.

She could hardly trust her ears, but sure enough, she heard what sounded like sleigh bells jingling in the driveway. ''I don't believe this.''

''Anybody around here own a sleigh?'' Tom asked as they followed his eager son toward the farmyard.

She was about to say no when she remembered Helen Ryan bringing her youngsters into the store a few weeks ago. While they were browsing, one of the boys had pointed to a photograph of a bobsled and announced that his daddy was building something like it.

Helen had explained that the kids complained so much about missing the conveniences of their former home in Chattanooga that their dad had promised them a special country treat this Christmas. He'd sent away for a kit via the Internet.

''I forgot,'' she said. ''Lew Ryan does carpentry work as a hobby. He decided to build something special for his kids.''

''I see,'' Tom sounded wistful. ''That's something we wouldn't have space for, even if I had time.''

They emerged to see a bright red sleigh sitting behind a team of horses. Lew had spared no luxury: the seats sported velvet cushions, and silvery bells studded the reins.

Lew and Helen sat in front with their daughter between them, while their sons traded playful jabs in the back. ''Merry Christmas!'' they called.

''I'm impressed.'' Tom grinned as he approached.

''We can't believe it snowed on Christmas Eve,'' Helen admitted. ''It's perfect!''

"Can I ride?" Cody gazed at Helen hopefully.

"I'm sure it can be arranged."

The front door flew open and the rest of Marnie's family piled out, fumbling with their coats. There were greetings and waves. Bonita's longing shone in her eyes, and so did Mike's.

"I'll be happy to give everyone a turn down the road," Lew said, and received an immediate chorus of acceptances. "With the snow so thick, there's no traffic to worry about."

"These old bones can do without being bounced around on metal runners," Jolene grumbled. "Why don't Helen and the kids come inside? We'll have cookies and hot cider."

"That sounds lovely," said her neighbor.

Leaving the baby with Jolene, Bonita and Mike and his parents got in the sleigh and rode blissfully out of sight. When they returned, Marnie joined Lew in the front.

On the backseat beside Tom, Cody clapped his mittened hands with glee. He exclaimed at the heat rising visibly from the horses' backs and giggled at the jangling when they started forward.

"Where's Guthrie?" Marnie asked as they glided down the driveway. Glancing back, she saw a muscle jump in Tom's jaw and wondered if he was jealous.

Didn't he know she wasn't interested in the man?

"He has company," Lew observed as they slid onto the road. He'd been right—there was no one else on the road, and nothing moved on the landscape, either. The woods on one side and rolling fields on the other stretched like a scene from a postcard.

"Company?" Marnie repeated.

"His girlfriend from Chattanooga showed up yesterday."

"I didn't know he had one," she said. "Are they engaged?"

"Ashley said she was too much of a city girl to live on a farm." Lew shook the reins and clucked, and the horses quickened their pace. "Guess she started missing him too much."

No wonder Guthrie had seemed lonely. Although Marnie had appreciated the prospect of a beau, she couldn't begrudge Guthrie a chance for happiness with someone who really loved him.

They rode for a while in silence, except for the jingle of bells and Cody's exclamations to, "Look, Daddy!" at just about everything.

Finally Lew spoke again. "If you don't mind, I'd like to cut this short and get inside. I'm a mite cold."

"Would you mind if I took the sleigh out for another turn?" Tom asked. "I'm good with horses."

"Don't mind at all," Lew said. "Take your time. I've got a feeling Guthrie would just as soon we stayed away for a few hours."

They pulled back into the farmyard and circled so that the horses faced the lane. When Lew got down, Tom handed him his son from the back. "I'm afraid he might get chilled," he said. "Would you do me a favor and take him inside?"

Marnie felt a prick of embarrassment. Everyone would know that she and Tom wanted some time together, and there would be speculation about it.

But he was leaving tomorrow. Besides, what could be more romantic than a sleigh ride together?

She would take all the memories she could get. At

least she would have them to treasure as long as she lived.

"I'd be glad to." Lew collected the little boy. "Come on, son. I hear there are cookies around here."

"Pat horsie?" Cody asked.

The farmer let him run his little hand over the nearest horse's curved neck, and then they went inside. Tom climbed into place beside Marnie.

"Alone at last," he joked, and shook the reins.

Chapter Fourteen

The whispering motion of the sleigh lulled Tom into another world. A world where he and Marnie existed apart from everyday realities, from other people's expectations, from the past and the future.

They floated between drifts of snow that transformed gulleys and rocks into a magical landscape. Hoofprints near the road revealed the recent approach of deer; the slightest flicker of wings among the trees exposed birds taking flight.

The leaden cloud cover began to break up, as forecast. Patches of blue sky appeared intermittently as the horses pushed beyond their previous trail onto virgin snow.

The sun came out, setting off an explosion of light that lent a dazzling sheen to the surface of the snow. This snow wouldn't last long, Tom thought. It was probably already melting. Did magic always have to be temporary?

For some reason Tom felt a need to draw closer to the old shack where he'd grown up. It held the key to his past and, perhaps, his future, and he wanted Marnie to understand.

A mile farther along, the horses were beginning to tire, and Tom was grateful to see that they'd reached the turnoff to the tangled grove. Without explanation, he stopped by the edge of the road.

Marnie, who had been silently gazing at the icy splendor around them, roused when he jumped out to turn the horses. "We're going back?"

"You have a better idea?" he teased. "Some hideaway I don't know about?"

She smiled dreamily. With her cheeks rosy from the brisk air and her hair sprouting wildly beneath her knitted cap, she looked like a merry soul from some Norse legend.

"I wish we could go on forever," she admitted. "But I'll bet the horses would beg to differ." At last she became aware of their surroundings. "Isn't this your old stomping grounds?"

He led the horses carefully around, making sure the radius wasn't sharp enough to tip the sleigh. "I'm afraid so."

"Is there some symbolic significance?" she asked. "Such as that you've decided to turn your life around?"

He laughed. "I thought we left that kind of heavy symbolism back at our college literature classes."

"What was that professor's name?" Marnie asked. "The one who saw a hidden meaning in everything?"

"All I remember is that you called him Professor Freud. Not to his face, of course."

"And you were so shocked!"

"Until I got used to being at university, I thought college professors were demigods."

"Unfortunately, some of them did, too," Marnie joked, and he joined in her mirth.

Those days had been some of the happiest of his life. Recalling them bolstered his determination to go on.

"Marnie, I did bring you here for a reason, so your comment about symbolism wasn't entirely wrong." He mounted the driver's seat and let the horses amble forward. "This place, much as I despise it, reminds me of who I am."

"Does it?" she asked. "By now, I should think it would remind you of who you used to be."

"In some ways." He ached to slip an arm around her. He wanted to taste her parted lips and hear her breath quicken. But there were more important matters at hand. "Coming back here yesterday helped me confront some truths about myself."

"Such as?" He couldn't blame her for the nervous quaver in her voice. Their quarrel last night must have convinced her that any changes in him hadn't been for the better.

"I'm not sure how to convey this, but here goes." He met her anxious gaze squarely. "Marnie, I love you desperately. But I have to be honest with you and with myself."

"I thought you always had been."

Snow crunched beneath the runners as the horses plodded on. "I have been, as far as I knew. All these years I've tried to deny who I am. To run away from it."

She wrapped her arms around herself protectively. "I guess I sensed that."

"I don't want to be like my father," Tom said. "Not anything like him."

"You aren't."

"Everything comes from somewhere." He pressed the point, eager to get his thoughts into the open. "I am what I've made of myself, but I'm also my parents' child. I have to accept that. Part of what drives me to succeed is the same darkness that drove my father toward self-destruction. I've just learned how to use it constructively." They reached a fork and he guided the horses along their own earlier tracks, in reverse.

"I suppose you must have some character traits in common," Marnie conceded at last. "Your dad, from what little I saw of him, had a forceful personality and a lot of energy. So do you."

"He wasted it on drinking and self-pity and violence," Tom said. "I've channeled that restlessness into my work. But I can't pretend it doesn't exist. I haven't tamed it, Marnie. It's still there and always will be."

As usual, she saw where he was leading. "You're trying to explain why you need to stay in the Foreign Service. Why you can't accept small-town life."

"That's right but..." Tom's diplomatic training warned him to phrase this delicately, although his instincts insisted on the direct approach. "Marnie, I love you. I keep hoping that you'll love me enough to marry me again, just the way I am, and move to Rome with Cody and me. Will you?"

Her teeth caught her lower lip, and moisture glittered against her thick lashes. Suddenly he knew what she was thinking, too. "You're wondering about children, aren't you?"

"I don't want to pick a fight," she said. "Whenever I bring up the subject, you get angry."

"I do?" He hadn't realized he was so touchy. "Marnie, I believe kids have a right to be wanted wholeheartedly. They need a community, friends, extended family. And parents who are willing to sacrifice for them. Cody happens to be unusually flexible, and together we're making the best of things. That doesn't mean all children would be that way."

"I want them so much." A tear ran down her cheek and etched itself into Tom's heart.

But if they weren't honest with each other, it could rip them apart later. "What if we had a child with medical problems? Or special talents that deserved developing? Wouldn't he deserve parents willing to adjust their lives for him? I'm not sure I could do that."

"People have to take life as it comes." Marnie's face reflected her uncertainty. "No one can control the future."

"Marnie, we love each other. The question is, how much?"

Her forehead furrowed. "What do you mean?"

"What it comes down to," Tom said, "is which do you want most—a husband who's willing to live in a small town and have kids, or me? I hope the answer is me."

She pressed her lips together so hard they paled. "Oh, Tom! Sometimes it's hard to believe we've been divorced for four years. You're such a part of me."

He waited, in torment, to hear what she would say next. Longing for her to say yes. Aware that he was asking her to give up a great deal.

She sighed. "Can I have some time to think about it?"

"Sure." He didn't need to point out that he would be leaving tomorrow; she was well aware of that. "I don't suppose you'd care to give me a hint?"

"You mean, of which way I'm inclining?"

"Exactly."

"I wish I knew," she said.

MARNIE HELD HERSELF stiffly in the cushioned seat. Tom had said he loved her and had asked her to marry him.

She loved him more than she could ever love anyone else, and true love was supposed to conquer all. But did she love him enough to sacrifice half her dreams?

When they pulled into the farmyard, she saw that the Ryan kids had tumbled outside and were showing Cody how to make snow angels by lying flat and waving their arms and legs. A once-clear area of the yard was covered with flat angel shapes and with children making more.

For an instant she imagined that these children were hers. That she had cradled each one as an infant and watched their first steps and heard their first words.

Would it ever fade, this longing for a baby? Did she dare risk the possibility that it wouldn't?

After she and Tom turned over the sleigh to Lew Ryan and watched his family glide away over the shining snow, they tramped inside with Cody. Most of the family had retired for a nap; Artie, however, remained glued to the computer screen.

He invited Cody to join him. The little boy yawned and said he would, then curled on the bed. Almost at once his eyes drifted shut.

Marnie had never heard of a two-year-old willingly lying down for a nap. She could see what Tom meant about the boy being easy to supervise.

They found Jolene in the kitchen, flipping through her recipe box. "It's about time you two got here," she said. "We need to get the turkey in the oven, or has everybody forgotten about Christmas dinner?"

Marnie had, actually. "I hope you weren't planning to eat early. There's no way it'll be done before six, even if we don't stuff it."

"Not stuff it?" Tom stared at her in mock horror. "I might as well go back to Italy today."

"Oh, piffle," said Jolene. "We'll make that instant dressing, and Tom can help me truss the thing."

Marnie was glad that her aunt and Bonita were resting, because there wasn't room in the kitchen for anyone else. Not the way she had to race around, pulling ingredients out of the pantry and dodging Tom and Granny as they worked over the bird like a pair of surgeons.

Soon the turkey was cleaned, stuffed and bristling with meat thermometers. Into the preheated oven it went, while Marnie peeled and cut up potatoes. They would sit in a pot of water until time to boil and mash them.

By then she was feeling tired and overheated. It was a relief when Linda appeared and, in compensation for abandoning turkey duty, declared that she would make the gravy and the sweet-potato casserole.

"I'd like you to check where I repaired the raccoon hole," Tom told Marnie. "Come upstairs with me?"

Since he didn't need anyone to inspect his carpentry, it was obvious he wanted to talk with her. Did he expect an answer so soon? Marnie hoped not, because she didn't have one to give him.

She didn't want to say so in front of the others, though, so she nodded and accompanied him. She could feel her grandmother's approval and Linda's speculation burning into her back.

Upstairs Tom excused himself and hurried to his room. When he emerged a moment later, Marnie couldn't help drinking in the sight of this handsome man striding toward her.

The sophisticated fit of his sweater and slacks emphasized the lean manliness of his body, and his eyes took on aqua depths in the shadowed hallway. He was both the boy she'd known and a man she hardly knew, Thomas Jakes, resident of Rome.

How dare she try to tie him to her apron strings in this tiny town, when he belonged on a vast stage? A shudder stirred by hunger and love and even a little awe ran through Marnie.

When Tom reached for her hand, he noticed that it was trembling. "What's wrong?"

"Nothing." She managed a smile. "I guess you just have that effect on me."

"Good." He slanted her a grin. "Now come upstairs and let's pretend we give a hoot about the darn raccoon."

They went up together into the early-afternoon

glare. Marnie had forgotten how warm the attic could become when the sun shone, even in winter.

The trunk remained open from this morning, with bits of stray glitter sparkling on the wooden floor. Except for that and a few boards nailed into one corner, however, there was no reminder of angels or animals.

"Now what's this all about?" Marnie demanded.

Tom assumed a boyish expression. "Why, Miss Afton, ah jes' want to be certain-sure ma work passes muster."

"You phony." Standing on tiptoe, she grabbed the front of his shirt above the V-neck sweater. "How gullible do you think I am?"

"Now, Miss Afton, ma'am," Tom continued in that wheedling voice, "anybody'd think you wanted me to do something like this." He brushed a kiss across her mouth. "Or this." He caught her shoulders and pulled her close.

"Why would they think that?" she mumbled, hoping he would kiss her again.

"They've got dirty minds from watching too much television." Looping one arm around her waist so she couldn't pull away, Tom surveyed her as if debating from which angle to launch the next tender assault. "Or maybe they read about it on the Internet."

"Read about what?" Marnie challenged.

"That danged French kissin'," he said, and proceeded to demonstrate.

The moment his tongue entered her mouth, Marnie felt her knees buckle. If it weren't for his arm around her, she would have collapsed.

She pressed upward, wanting more. Her palm

stroked his cheek, feeling a hint of bristle fighting its way to the surface.

A yearning fired through her to awaken every morning and touch his rough cheek. To be his true intimate, his wife, once again.

His hands caressed her rib cage, and with a gasp she felt his thumbs stroke her breasts through the denim fabric of her dress. Her breasts grew ripe, and heat flared into her core.

"Tom," she whispered.

He groaned deep in his throat. "This is going to drive me crazy."

"We can't do anything here."

"I know." Swallowing hard, he stepped back a few inches. "Believe it or not, this isn't why I lured you up here."

Marnie wanted him so badly at this moment that she would have agreed to almost anything, but she hoped he wasn't going to renew his proposal. Not while she was so vulnerable.

He didn't. Instead, he reached into his pocket and pulled out a red velvet jeweler's box. "I wanted to give you your birthday present."

"My birthday's in April," she couldn't resist pointing out.

"I know that." He was standing so close that his breath tickled her cheek. "But I missed the last one. The last several ones, in fact. Remember how I always wanted to give you your birthstone as a gift?"

That would be diamonds, which he'd never been able to afford, except for the small ones in her wedding ring. He flipped open the box. Nestled there lay two sleek gold earrings set with diamonds of such clarity that they danced with rainbows.

Marnie realized Tom must have spent a fortune on them. "They're incredibly beautiful."

"I hope you don't mind the modern design," he said. "The Italians are very up-to-date, but I could exchange them for something more traditional."

"I like the simplicity." Marnie scarcely dared touch them.

"These are for all the birthdays I missed." His voice tantalized her ear. "And the Christmases. I want you to have them, no matter what you decide."

She had never cared much for flashy jewelry, but these diamonds were different. Pure and elegant, and a sign of Tom's genuine caring. He'd selected this before the two of them met again or held each other or went to bed.

He'd done it simply because he wanted to. The fact that he wasn't trying to influence her made the gift even more precious to Marnie.

Seeing her hesitation, Tom set the jeweler's box on a shelf and removed one of the earrings. "Duck your head a little. There."

He fastened the earring in place. The gesture reminded her how much he had enjoyed zipping and buttoning her into her clothes in the morning, even brushing her hair. He had gentle, skillful hands.

"Now the other one." She swiveled obediently and felt him fix it in her lobe. It was as if he'd marked her for his own.

Downstairs the phone rang. It must be someone calling to wish them a happy holiday, Marnie thought. She felt no inclination whatsoever to find out who.

Scarcely daring to breathe, she approached the old mirror. The antique glass softened everything like a sepia photograph, making her eyes appear large and glowing. The earrings flashed as she turned her head to examine them.

From behind Tom gathered her close, his chin resting atop her head, his chest bracing her. "I tried to picture how they would look on you, but I didn't do you justice. Marnie, you have an inner fire that illuminates everything around you."

How could she not marry this man when she loved him so much? She had to be with him, no matter what it cost.

"Tom—"

Another voice overlaid her own. It was Jolene's voice from downstairs, calling, "Tom!" with a note of concern.

"I'd better see what's up." Reluctantly he released her and went to the head of the stairs. "Yes?"

Stairs creaked, and Mike came bounding from below. "Dr. Spindler got an urgent call to look in on one of Dr. Rosen's patients in town. He's concerned about his reflexes, driving that far in the snow. I offered my services but he wants you."

"Of course I'll drive." Tom glanced questioningly at Marnie.

"I'll come, too." She wanted to stay near him.

They found Artie fastening on his coat. His usually jovial face was creased with worry. "Thanks, Tom. I'm pretty self-sufficient, but I've got a feeling this snow is going to turn to ice, and I don't trust myself."

"I don't mind," Tom said so gallantly that, had

Marnie not known better, she would have believed him.

Jolene watched them pull their coats from the rack. "Looks like it's a good thing that turkey won't be done till late."

The doctor glanced at Marnie. "You sure you want to come? It's bad enough for two men to risk getting stuck in a snowdrift. And it appears Mrs. Lattimore's broken her hip, which means I may have to admit her to the hospital. It could take hours."

Marnie brushed aside the concerns. "If the rest of you don't mind taking charge of dinner, I'd like to go. Tom could use the company."

"We don't mind at all," Linda said.

"Sorry." Artie gazed apologetically at Jolene. "I knew I was on call, but I didn't mean to spoil your day."

"You're not spoilng it," she said. "I just hope Mrs. Lattimore's not seriously hurt."

"We'll pray for her," promised Norbert.

The doctor's sport utility vehicle was high off the ground, and its heavy tires plowed easily through the slushy snow as they set off. Marnie sat in back to give Artie and Tom a chance to talk.

The sun shone with unseemly vigor, and melting snow dripped from the trees. She was relieved to notice growing dark patches on the ground, an indication that the snow was indeed vanishing.

She only hoped they didn't get a freeze tonight. The roads would turn to ice.

"Mrs. Lattimore was one of my longtime patients, before I sold the practice," Artie told them as they swung onto the road. "Her daughter said she fell in the bathroom."

"You said she broke her hip?" Marnie prompted.

"Apparently." He sighed. "An injury like that can indicate osteoporosis—bone thinning. I hope it doesn't, because that's a nasty, crippling disease some women get as they age."

"Granny doesn't have it?" Marnie leaned forward to hear better.

He shook his head. "Fortunately she listens to my nagging. She goes for a walk every day, weather permitting, takes calcium supplements and uses progesterone cream."

"I'm glad Granny has you." The snow forced Tom to proceed at about half the usual speed, and he kept his gaze fixed on the road.

"That woman's as healthy as they come." Artie ruffled one hand through his thick white hair. "I apologize for letting her buffalo you folks about her heart condition. She'd have had my head if I didn't go along."

Tom's grip tightened on the wheel. "Frankly, I'm grateful. If it hadn't been for what she said, I might have talked myself out of coming for Christmas. That would have been a major mistake."

With a rush Marnie remembered how he'd been holding her before they were interrupted. Instinctively she touched the earrings he'd presented so lovingly.

The doctor noticed them, too. "Pretty sparklers. Are those new?"

"Very new," she said.

"Diamonds are forever," he murmured. Neither of them responded.

When they reached town, Artie directed them toward Mrs. Lattimore's house. "This could take a while," he warned. "Even if she's not badly hurt, she's pretty shaken up."

"We'll wait at my house," Marnie volunteered.

"Like I said, it could take hours," Artie warned. "You might want to drive around and look at the decorations."

"We'll figure something out." Tom handed him a card. "You can call us on my cell phone."

The doctor must have noticed the gleam in his eye, because he added, "You'll figure something out? Of course you will! I sound like a complete old fool."

"Not at all," Tom said with deliberate blandness. Marnie was blushing so hard she didn't trust herself to speak.

They stopped at a one-story brick house, dark red against the snowy yard. Tom waited until the doctor was ushered inside, then backed out of the driveway.

"Your house," he murmured to Marnie, who had moved to the seat beside him. "Now why does that sound like the best place in the universe to me?"

She didn't need to answer. Her own rapid pulse told her why.

Chapter Fifteen

Inside Marnie's house the soft colors and the profusion of teddy bears gave the living room a welcoming quality. Tom felt cocooned against the chill and the gathering twilight.

He inhaled a trace of flowers and felt a pleasant buzz in his veins. The rooms were infused with a sensual aura as if some essence of Marnie had become part of the very air. At every level he was aware that the two of them had come here alone.

They exchanged idle comments about the doctor and the snow as they shed their coats and damp shoes. When Marnie pulled off her knit cap, her brown hair fell in rumpled curls around her face. A healthy pink flushed her skin, and she met his eyes shyly.

Tom enjoyed seeing how the diamonds gleamed against her earlobes. If he had his way, he would shower her with beautiful things.

"Marry me, woman," he said.

She took a shuddering breath. "Yes."

He couldn't believe what he'd heard. "Yes?"

She nodded.

Tom had known the satisfaction of earning his college diploma and the thrill of marrying Marnie the first time. But what he felt now was both more profound and more subtle.

It was the startling sense that life might really give him what he wanted most. That happiness was attainable, when he'd believed it irretrievably lost.

His skin shimmered with a sensitivity that made it almost painful to touch her. Instead, he placed his palms on her shoulders and ran them along her arms.

She uttered a little gasp. "I can't believe how good that feels."

He loved the way her lips parted and her brown eyes got darker. "There's more where that came from."

"Promises, promises." The light tone stuck in her throat.

It was like a dance, this hesitation between them. A dramatic pause in the tango as they waited for the beat to sweep them away.

Bending, Tom brushed his lips across Marnie's. She reached for him, and he lifted her with one swoop. The waiting was over.

Holding her in his arms, he carried her up the stairs as she clung to him. She felt lighter than he would have believed; his adrenaline was pounding full force. In fact, he was stirring to life all over.

He wanted intensely to make love to her in her own bed, to imprint himself on this place and on the life she led. To integrate himself into them until she could no longer tell the difference.

Tom's feelings for Marnie went far beyond the sexual, but he would never deny the power of that side of his masculinity. And she aroused it like no one else.

Upstairs, he eased her onto her four-poster bed. Outside, the daylight might be fading, yet he felt no need to turn on a lamp. Sensations much stronger than sight packed the room.

He buried his face in Marnie's hair, reveling in its feathery softness. Her arms surrounded him, and her breasts yielded beneath his chest, tantalizing him with their tight nubs.

It was like their wedding night all over again, except this time they weren't inexperienced, fumbling newlyweds but a man and woman who understood passion in its deepest sense. The confirmation of love, the promise of forever.

Marnie slid her hands beneath his sweater and began unbuttoning his shirt. Tom could hardly contain himself, and yet he wanted to linger, to enjoy every minute and make it special for her.

Supporting himself on one elbow, he eased down Marnie's tights and caressed her thighs beneath the denim dress. A whisper of desire escaped her, and then she pulled up his sweater and bent to trace her lips across his hard stomach.

Sensations blazed through him, and he became acutely attuned to the rhythmic response of her body beneath his stroking. When she came up for air, Tom saw that Marnie's face was alight with happiness. She caught his head in her hands, and her tongue burrowed into his mouth, stirring embers until they crackled into open flame.

There were too many clothes between them: the hardness of his belt, the fabric of her smock and his pants, yet he couldn't tear himself away from kissing her long enough to remove them.

Marnie opened her mouth as if to speak, but Tom refused to let her. Instead, he kissed her again. At the same time his hands roved over her hips, pulling up her dress as she unworked his belt. Then, she pulled off his shirt and sweater and tossed them aside.

With a low groan, he positioned her atop him. Against his bare chest, he could feel the eagerness of her movements and knew she must be intimately aware of his arousal, pressing into her core.

When she eased downward, he wanted to protest, but she was doing something below his waist, removing his pants, claiming his masculinity and encouraging it to savage readiness. Pleasure lashed at Tom, made all the keener by the rippling undercurrent of tenderness.

He grasped Marnie's crumpled denim smock. Marnie gave a helpful twist and the whole dress lifted away. A few fumblings later, he tossed her underwear after it.

Tom pressed his palms against her bare nipples. A quiver ran through her, and her eyes closed blissfully.

"Don't stop what you were doing," he said hoarsely.

"I wouldn't dream of it." She bent again to take him in her mouth. He had never felt anything so intense, so overwhelming.

If he let her continue, his climax would seize him too quickly. He wanted to bring Marnie with him, every step of the way.

"Enough," he rasped.

Obediently she balanced above him, lusciously

nude, her sweet face poised over his. "I thought you didn't want me to stop."

"Woman, you drive me crazy." He reached for her hips with pretended languor and, at the same time, licked lightly upward, catching the points of her breasts.

Instinctively she arched over him. Unable to refrain even a millisecond longer, he thrust into her with one fierce stroke.

Marnie cried out in pleasure. Tom reveled in the vibrations that rocked her self-control, until his own need would wait no longer.

Like a rod of fire, it overpowered him with its white heat. Wave after wave pulsed through him, seared him, melted him into Marnie.

His soaring climax stimulated her to new heights. As he reached his peak, so did she. He could feel it in the quivers that gripped her and hear it in her soft noises and smell the wonderful richness of the two of them becoming one.

The fire receded gradually. Marnie relaxed beside him, her head resting on his shoulder.

Tom hadn't known such sheer happiness since the early days of their marriage. Maybe never, because now his contentment shone all the brighter in contrast to the loneliness of the past four years.

She loved him, fully and completely. She was going to marry him, and he'd never let her go again.

Outside, the moon rose, lightening the room. It illuminated the photo montage on the wall, giving Tom the impression that all those special occasions—her childhood, their college graduation, their wedding—were coalescing into this moment.

Tonight the impurities of his life had been burned away by the heat of their passion. Their lovemaking was different from before. Freer, more intense.

Then he suddenly realized he'd forgotten to use a condom. It was the first time they'd had intercourse without some form of protection.

Until this moment he hadn't given the matter a thought. Neither, he felt certain, had Marnie.

To his surprise there was no panic, none of the sense of a trap closing that he usually experienced whenever she expressed a wish for children. Here, with his dearest memories close by and his wife in his arms, nothing frightened him.

Not that he had been afraid before. Had he?

"Marnie?" He shifted her closer. "I forgot to use protection."

"It's all right," her voice murmured through the silvery air. "It's the wrong time of the month."

He should have been relieved. Instead he felt almost let down, and somewhat confused. "Last night you made such a big deal about not wanting to use anything."

"I wasn't trying to get pregnant." Her breath warmed his cheek. "I just wanted all of you, with nothing between us."

Regret washed over Tom, that he'd misinterpreted her so harshly. "I'm sorry. I jumped to conclusions."

"Well, it looks like I got my way after all, doesn't it?"

He chuckled. "In a way we both did."

A heartbeat later she rolled away from him. "Dr. Spindler should be calling soon. We'd better get dressed."

"Any century now." He didn't want to leave this cozy nest any sooner than he had to.

Lazily he watched Marnie sit up, her hair tumbling around her shoulders. The bed shifted as she stood, and cool air currents drifted over his heated skin as she put on her underclothes and dress.

He loved watching her. It was a pleasure that had never faded in their six years of marriage, and he doubted it ever would.

When she left the room to finish getting ready, he dragged himself out of bed and dressed slowly. Tom hated to leave this place. He'd never had such a strong sense of home anywhere else, except at Jolene's farm.

Maybe they could keep the house and come back to visit. The prospect of anyone else living here bothered him.

While he was brushing his hair, he heard Marnie emerge from the bathroom and walk down the hall. A light clicked on, its glow faintly visible from where he stood.

What was she doing? Why hadn't she come back here?

When Tom stepped into the hall, he realized she'd gone into the nursery. Curious, he walked toward it.

Marnie stood with her back to him, facing the oak crib. The puppies and kittens on the wallpaper pranced motionlessly around her.

As he watched, she straightened her shoulders. It was as if she'd been saying goodbye.

When she turned, he saw a glimmer of tears in her eyes. She flicked off the light so quickly, though, that he couldn't be sure.

More than anything in the world, Tom didn't want to risk changing her mind about coming with him. But he couldn't let her walk into the future with half a heart.

"Are you sure?" he asked.

"What?" Her face lifted in the dimness. Her eyes were like dark pools.

"About marrying me?" He could barely get the words out.

She nodded.

"You don't look sure," he said.

"You didn't believe that I loved you enough, just for yourself. But I do, Tom. I only wish—" She stopped.

He yearned to take her in his arms, but sensed that she needed her distance or she might never finish explaining. "Wish what?"

"That you loved me enough to want children with me." The words came out with a small sob at the end.

He couldn't believe it. "Is that what you think?" This time he yielded to his urge and gathered her close. "Marnie, my feelings about kids have nothing to do with you. This is the way I am. But I can't be myself without you. I need you."

"I love you." Against his neck he could feel the tears coursing down her cheeks. "I want to be with you."

"Always," he vowed. "We'll always be together. Don't ever leave me again."

"I won't," she promised. But she was still crying.

Downstairs he heard the muffled sound of his cell phone ringing. Darn, he'd left it in his coat!

Tom was tempted to ignore it. "Marnie..."

"Go on!" She ducked away. "I'm fine."

"You're not!"

"Get the phone!"

He knew she was right. Irrationally annoyed at the interruption, he hurried down the stairs.

Much as he relished the latest technological achievements, Tom understood why some people wished the phone had never been invented. As he reached the front closet and fumbled in his coat pocket, he would easily have consigned Alexander Graham Bell to outer darkness.

At last he located the infernal thing and got it to his ear. "Yes?"

It was Artie, of course. At least he brought good news. Mrs. Lattimore had only bruised her hip, and a mild painkiller had restored her enough to enjoy the rest of Christmas.

The doctor was ready to be picked up. Time to go and eat their own Christmas dinner.

"We'll be right there," Tom said.

Distractedly he met Marnie at the foot of the stairs. He needed a chance to absorb what she'd said. Maybe he'd been thick-headed, but it had never occurred to him that she might interpret his insistence on remaining child free as a rejection of her. Yet she'd loved him enough to say yes, anyway. To come back and make him happy and to accept his child as her own.

She was giving him the greatest Christmas present of all—unconditional love.

It was what he'd always craved. Now he had to ask himself, Tom realized as he helped her into her coat, whether he was offering her the same.

ON THE RETURN TRIP Dr. Spindler told them how relieved he was about his elderly patient, who might have faced serious consequences if she'd actually broken her hip.

Marnie was grateful that Artie chatted nonstop, because she didn't feel like talking. Neither, apparently, did Tom. Through the windshield, the headlights barely made a dent in the darkness, and she guessed that it took all of his concentration to steer through the slushy snow.

In the backseat, she made appropriate responses to the doctor, but she was only half listening. Although her body glowed with contentment, Marnie's mind was in turmoil.

Making love to Tom in her bedroom had meant even more than she'd expected. Her house had been purchased as a refuge from a broken marriage, but now she could see that the only way either of them could heal was to mend the marriage itself.

They belonged together. She couldn't and wouldn't fight it any longer.

Still, it was going to be difficult to leave. She'd grown attached to the house, or at least to her fantasies about the future she might enjoy there.

She would have to leave the furnishings behind, just as the former owners had done. A Foreign Service family had to keep its possessions to a minimum.

What family would buy the house and come to live there? Marnie would prefer a young couple, so the nursery wouldn't go to waste. That darling little crib should hold a newborn, even if it couldn't be hers.

Her chest squeezed. She couldn't deny a sense of

loss. But surely it would dim as she began her new life with Tom and Cody.

Then there was the prospect of selling the bookstore. What about the shipments she'd ordered for a Valentine's Day display? And the local teachers who consulted her about supplemental materials?

Well, surely Tom didn't expect her to leave with him tomorrow; her passport wasn't even current. In the months ahead, while they planned their wedding, she would have time to put her business affairs in order.

Certainly she didn't regret saying yes. It had been, and would always be, the right decision.

They turned into the farmyard. The three-story house blazed with lights, inside and out. Against the stark, charcoal countryside, the colored holiday strands provided a faerie touch.

"It looks like a setting from a classic film," Tom observed. "One of those old Jimmy Stewart movies."

"It's better. First of all, it's in color. Besides, they didn't have Sniff-o-rama, did they?" The doctor patted his stomach. "I can smell dinner cooking all the way out here."

Marnie could, too. Apple pie and stuffing and sweet-potato casserole. Well, maybe she couldn't detect all those scents, but a hint of cinnamon and a whiff of roasting turkey was enough. Her imagination supplied the rest.

Tom parked and they stumped across the yard toward the porch. The pale moon played tricks around them, creating illusory patterns of shadow and clarity. The snow angels shimmered faintly, as if they were moving, and Marnie wondered whether, to the man in the moon, they looked real.

Inside, Granny and Aunt Linda came to greet them, eager for news of Mrs. Lattimore. In the living room Mike was playing Monopoly Junior with Cody. The little boy couldn't keep track of the rules, so Bonita was helping him while Baby Josie napped on a blanket on the floor.

The peaceful scene filled Marnie with an emotion beyond nostalgia—a sense of the rightness of things and an awareness of how quickly such precious moments passed.

She glanced at Tom and found he was regarding the others with a quizzical expression. Perhaps, like her, he hesitated to make public what had transpired between the two of them.

Not that their reconciliation was a secret, but she wanted to keep the news private a little while longer. To treasure it for herself, like a shiny new toy on Christmas day that she wasn't ready to let anyone else play with.

"You're just in time to put the food on the table," Granny announced from behind her. "Let's get cracking!"

"I'm starved," said Artie. "What can I do?"

"Me, too." Marnie pitched in willingly. There seemed to be endless bowls and dishes and platters to carry from the kitchen.

Where had all this food come from, anyway? She had seen some of it in the pantry and refrigerator, and had helped prepare the turkey earlier, but Granny must have kept some items in the freezer on the screened back porch and in the root cellar.

To the menu had been added green beans topped with almonds, carrot-raisin salad and fruit ambrosia. There were also three kinds of cranberry sauce, and whole-wheat rolls.

"We've been busy," Linda said, seeing her reaction.

"I'm impressed," Marnie admitted. "Sorry I wasn't here to help."

"Oh, that's all right." Her aunt dusted her hands and went to take off her apron. From her tone of voice she'd left much unsaid.

Marnie guessed that her aunt and grandmother had indulged in speculation regarding her departure with Tom. None of them believed in mean-spirited gossip, but that was different from taking an interest in the happiness of loved ones.

They would all be thrilled when they learned the truth. Marnie could picture the twinkle in Granny's eyes and the pleasure on her aunt's face. She hoped they wouldn't make comments about expecting more children in the family, though, because she didn't know how she would respond.

Jolene knew why Marnie had left Tom. But she'd pooh-poohed his refusal to have children, saying, "Why, he's a family man if there ever was one." And Cody's existence had proven her right. Or so the others must believe.

Soon food nearly overflowed the sideboard. Norbert put the turkey on the table in front of him, and they all sat down to pray.

Thank you for loved ones at Christmas…

Marnie sneaked a glance at Tom. His head was bowed, and she couldn't see his expression.

…for Thy bounty and goodness…

Cody squinted at a dish of black olives, took a quick look around and snagged one between his thumb and forefinger. When he thought no one was watching, he popped it in his mouth.

…for peace and for freedom…

The baby let out a burp. Bonita and Mike both peeked to make sure she was all right. Their gazes locked, and for a second Marnie could have sworn they forgot anyone else was in the room.

…for old friends and new…

With his face downturned, Dr. Spindler looked like a big shock of white hair above folded hands. Why hadn't he asked Granny to marry him? Marnie wondered. The two of them seemed perfectly suited.

Perhaps he was contented just to see her once in a while. Marnie knew her grandmother would like more, but Jolene wasn't the type to moon over a man. Not even one with a cute rear end.

Amen.

Around the table, people stirred. "Merry Christmas!" "Merry Christmas!"

"Can we eat now?" asked Cody.

Tom smiled. "He certainly gets to the point, doesn't he?"

"Why shouldn't he?" demanded Granny. "Are you going to let that little boy starve?"

The others followed Cody and Tom to the buffet. Getting in line with plate in hand, Mike said, "I think we ought to invite that poor raccoon. I mean, look at all this food!"

"Why not the cat, too?" teased his mother.

"Kitty eat with us?" Cody asked hopefully as his father piled food on his plate.

"He was joking, dear," Linda said. "At least, I hope so."

Marnie let the others go ahead. The food smelled wonderful, but she wasn't as hungry as she'd expected. Watching her family's small, loving interactions filled her with such buoyant happiness that there was scarcely room for anything else.

At last she filled her plate and took her seat beside Tom. He finished cutting Cody's food and touched her hand lightly.

Quiet fell as people tucked into their dinners. Marnie could hear the fire crackle in the living room.

From their point of contact, she felt the deep rumble of Tom's voice as he broke into the comfortable silence. "Folks? Sorry to interrupt, but I have something important to say."

He'd said, "I," not "we." And it wasn't like him to make public announcements. Was he simply carried away by excitement about their engagement?

Jolene looked up, a forkful of sweet potatoes in her hand. Norbert regarded Tom with pastoral concern.

"It strikes me that Christmas is a time to open our hearts," Tom continued. "And I feel like I'm part of this family. So I beg your indulgence if I speak bluntly."

"Go right ahead, Tom," Linda said.

He took a deep breath. "I know this will come as a surprise to Marnie, but I've realized that I was about to make the biggest mistake of my life."

Chapter Sixteen

Marnie struggled to catch her breath. Could he possibly have changed his mind about marrying her?

Besides, she couldn't believe he meant to humiliate her in front of her family. But why hadn't he prepared her for whatever he was going to say?

It was clearly no joke. Tom's blue eyes had narrowed, and a muscle twitched in his jaw. She recognized the signs of intense concentration.

Around the table everyone waited. Twisting her cloth napkin in her hands, she forced herself to sit still.

"Earlier today I proposed to Marnie and she did me the honor of accepting." Now Tom had the undivided attention of everyone except Cody, who was finger feeding himself green beans. "In case you're wondering, that isn't the mistake I was referring to."

"I should hope not!" harrumphed Jolene. The tightness in Marnie's chest eased, but only a little.

His gaze swept the table. "By the time a man reaches the age of thirty-two, he figures he knows himself pretty darn well. But that isn't necessarily true."

"Well, piffle," said Jolene. "I could have told you that."

"I wouldn't have believed you. As far as I was concerned, nobody could tell me anything." The candelabra made a twinkle appear in Tom's eye. "I figured I had my head on straight and it was going to stay that way."

"Straight?" Jolene's freckles quivered. "Letting Marnie leave you? That was a blockhead thing to do, if you don't mind my saying so."

"I don't mind, because it's true." A slow grin warmed his face. "Do you know why I let her go?"

"Some nonsense about not wanting children," Jolene said. Linda nodded; she had obviously heard the whole story from her mother.

"You don't want children?" Bonita's gaze went to Cody. "But—" She stopped at a signal from her husband.

"It's a long story," Tom continued, looking at everyone but Marnie. "I believed I was by nature an adventurer who couldn't bear to be tied down. I demanded that the woman I love accept me exactly as I was, warts and all."

"What are warts?" asked Cody.

His father patted his hand. "I'll tell you later."

Marnie couldn't contain herself any longer. "Would you please get to the point?"

When Tom turned to her, she saw regret in his blue gaze. "The prospect of having kids made me feel trapped. As if you were trying to force me into a mold that didn't fit. But now—" he lifted his hands in a carefree gesture "—it's gone."

"What is?"

"The fear," he said. "It's as if I took off a pair of sunglasses and suddenly I could see. I realized that I'm not really an adventurer. It's who I used to be, or perhaps who I needed to be at one time in my life. But not anymore."

"It's about time you came to your senses!" said Jolene. "Globe hopping like that is all very well for a while, but a man has to settle down sooner or later!"

"Jolene!" Playfully, Tom mimicked the exasperated tone Marnie adopted when her grandmother pushed her too hard. "I'd like to say this in my own way, please!"

Jolene turned to Artie. "He's a bit slow on the uptake, isn't he? For being so smart, I mean."

"I don't understand," Marnie said. "Tom, you know I intend to marry you, no matter whether you want children or not. But...do you?"

The buzz that had arisen among her relatives faded to silence. Mike and her grandmother stared at them as if watching a favorite soap opera.

Tom didn't give a direct answer. "I've been my own worst enemy," he said. "Growing up, I never felt that I was loved completely, just as I was. That lack must have festered inside me, coloring the way I perceived everything, even my marriage. Well, today you gave me the greatest gift of all, Marnie— unconditional love. It turned my world around."

The only sound in the room was the baby's soft cooing. Marnie discovered she was clutching the edges of her chair as if she might fall off.

"At first I couldn't understand why the idea of having more children didn't alarm me." Thank goodness

Tom refrained from going into detail about the situation that had arisen this afternoon when they forgot to use protection. "In fact, the more I thought about it, the more I dreaded leaving here tomorrow, even though I knew you would soon be joining me."

Marnie itched for him to cut to the chase. "Well? Why is that?"

Prying her hand from the chair, Tom cradled it in his. "There's nothing left for me to prove, to myself or anyone else. Being a husband and a father is all the adventure I need."

Even Cody seemed to grasp that something important was taking place. He stopped playing with his beans and regarded his father expectantly.

Marnie still didn't dare believe that all her dreams could come true. "You want kids? And you're even willing to stay in Ryder's Crossing?"

"Yes."

"You might change your mind."

"Never." Contentment softened Tom's voice. "When your uncle counted our blessings, it helped me see what really matters. The little things, the everyday things, the people around us."

The joy welling inside Marnie was almost too keen to bear. "This is happening so fast. Maybe you should think it over."

Tom shook his head. "Actually, I'm pretty impatient, now that I finally got my act together. Look how many years I've wasted! I want our kids to have the childhood I missed, one full of love. And I want to be part of a community where I can make a real difference. I'm ready to come home, Marnie."

Normally he was the one who had difficulty expressing his emotions. Now she found herself struggling for words.

She'd waited so long for this moment. Her throat clamped shut, although she wasn't sure whether it was clogged with laughter or tears.

He touched her cheek. "Will you forgive me for making you miserable? For being too arrogant to admit you knew me better than I knew myself?"

"I..." The words refused to come out. Marnie gestured helplessly.

"I don't believe it," Jolene said. "My granddaughter is too choked up to talk. I never thought I'd see the day!"

Tom took Marnie's hands. "Forgive me."

Forgive him? There was nothing to forgive, Marnie thought.

"I love you," she said.

"I love you, too," he said.

To her chagrin, hot tears spilled down her cheeks.

"Uh-oh." Tom pulled her onto his lap. "Looks like I made my wife cry."

Jolene stood up and grabbed her plate. "If everyone's done eating, let's clear so we can have dessert."

"Whoa!" Dr. Spindler raised his hands in protest. "Sit down, woman!"

"You offering to clear?" she demanded.

"I have a better idea," he said. "Tom has inspired me."

Instinctively, Jolene's hand flew to her new necklace. From the set of her grandmother's mouth, however, Marnie could tell she didn't want to get her hopes up.

"He said some fine words," Artie went on.

"About making people miserable, and needing to be forgiven."

"Well, I forgive you," she said tartly. "Now get on with it."

A bit taken aback, the doctor coughed. "I guess, I, uh, have been wanting to ask you but, uh, not knowing how, so, uh…"

She folded her arms. "Isn't that just like the man? You have to poke him with a stick to get the words out!"

The doctor snorted. "Well, you know what I'm trying to say!"

Jolene's mouth twisted wryly. "I'm waiting."

"For what?"

Tom caught Artie's eye and mouthed the word, "Love."

"Oh, right," said the older man. "I, er, love you."

"You sure do," she said. "The question is, Dr. Spindler, whether you love me enough to get down on your knees."

He sputtered. "On my knees? Jolene Afton, just forget this nonsense and promise to marry me!"

"That's close enough," she said and, as usual, got the last word. To everyone's delight, it was "Yes!"

Chapter Seventeen

"Don't worry! Tom will be thrilled," Betty said as she picked a bit of lint from Marnie's rose-colored dress. They had just finished dressing in the choir room at the church.

"I wish I could be sure." Marnie struggled to quell the sinking feeling in her stomach. It might come from nerves or…

She stared at herself in the mirror. Her eyes were large and luminous, her hair—thanks to an hour at the salon this morning—perfectly curled beneath its wreath of flowers.

As for the dress, its soft color brought out the radiance in her skin. Even more important, the lacy bodice and silky, body-skimming fabric disguised the growing roundness of her figure. "I should have told him."

"Too late to worry about that now." Standing to one side, her friend straightened her own light-pink matron-of-honor dress. Although Betty was taller and stouter, the two blended well because, after twenty years of friendship, they instinctively mirrored each other's movements. "Besides, you said it wasn't the sort of thing you wanted to discuss over the phone."

"That's true," Marnie said. "But I figured we'd have at least a couple of days before the ceremony to talk privately."

Four months ago, right after Christmas, Tom had returned to Rome with Cody to fulfill his work obligations. At the end of January, Marnie had suffered what she mistook for a touch of the flu.

Preoccupied with wedding plans and her work at the store, she hadn't bothered to schedule a checkup for another month. Then, since Artie was semi-retired, she'd gone to see young Dr. Rosen.

She'd stared at the dark-blue test strip in shock. "It can't be! It was the wrong time of the month!"

Dr. Rosen had smiled sympathetically. "That's a common misconception, no pun intended. Ovulation isn't as predictable as people think."

Tom had said he wanted children. But, deep inside, did he really? And so soon?

His overseas phone calls had tended to be short and rushed, with Cody chattering on the extension. Finding it impossible to talk to Tom alone, Marnie had tried to put her news in an e-mail, but couldn't get the words right.

He'd been scheduled to arrive several days before the wedding, and she'd counted on having time for a leisurely discussion. However, a high-level economic conference was announced at the last minute, taxing the embassy staff and forcing Tom to postpone his departure.

He and Cody didn't reach Ryder's Crossing until yesterday afternoon. They'd gone right to a tuxedo fitting at the tailor shop run by Betty's husband, Stewart.

Last night, Norbert had conducted a brief wedding rehearsal in her grandmother's living room. Afterward, a worn-out Cody insisted on sleeping with his father, and Marnie, exhausted, had fled home with her secret unrevealed.

At least she'd managed to keep anyone else from finding out, even Granny and Artie. They'd been mercifully distracted by their elopement last month to Las Vegas, followed by a two-week honeymoon.

Only Betty, who saw Marnie daily at the store, had guessed the truth. It was the morning nausea and frequent trips to the bathroom that gave her away.

So here she was, uneasily wishing she'd gotten this over with sooner. From the sanctuary drifted the scent of flowers and the bustle of friends and relatives as they took their seats. Talk about waiting until the last minute!

Her stomach churning, Marnie lowered herself into a chair. "I hope I'm not going to throw up."

"I thought you were past that stage!" Betty handed her a glass of water.

She took it gingerly, without removing her short white gloves. "So did I. Oh, Betty, I know it's bad luck for the groom to see the bride in her wedding dress, but I've got to talk to him before the ceremony!"

"Just cover it with something." Betty sifted through the lost-and-found garments on a long rack and handed her the ugliest raincoat Marnie had ever seen. "Put this on!"

"It's gross!"

"It'll hide your dress," retorted her friend. "Stay here. I'll go get Tom."

Marnie pressed her hands to her hot cheeks. "Be discreet! Don't scare him! Don't make people think I changed my mind or anything!"

"What kind of nincompoop do you take me for?" hooted Betty, and marched out of the room.

TOM HAD NOTICED an unaccustomed air of reserve about Marnie yesterday, and wished he'd had a chance to speak to her. He hoped his last-minute delay hadn't made her doubt his commitment to their new life.

Yes, he had enjoyed circulating among important people, using his skills to handle the thousand and one details required to make a conference come off smoothly. At the same time he'd become more and more aware of the fact that no one was indispensable, except to the family that loved him.

He'd missed Marnie so deeply that he wondered how he had survived for four years without her. He couldn't wait until they were married again.

Now that the moment had nearly come, he could barely control his impatience. The minutes ticked by with agonizing slowness in the minister's study, where Tom waited with Norbert and Cody.

The boy was happily showing off the ring he carried on a velvet cushion. Tom had faxed Marnie sketches of several rings, and she'd faxed back her preference and her ring size. Not exactly the most romantic way to handle such an important decision, Tom supposed, but it couldn't be helped.

A rap on the door roused him. When he saw Betty,

Tom's confusion deepened. He'd been expecting Mike, who was serving as his best man.

"I know this is a little unusual," Betty said, "but Marnie wants to talk to you."

A spurt of alarm speeded up Tom's heartbeat. It took all his diplomatic training to maintain a calm exterior. "Is something wrong?"

"No," Betty assured him. "I'd suggest you come with me, though."

"Sure." He could see he wasn't going to get any further information from their old friend. "Where is she?"

"This way."

"Is there anything I can do?" Norbert asked.

"Nope," Betty said. "Just watch Cody."

"I'll be glad to."

This church had been built since Tom left town, and he was grateful that the matron of honor knew a circuitous route that spared them the curious gazes of their guests. It also bypassed the vestibule where Jolene waited with Artie; Marnie had invited them both to walk her down the aisle.

The choir room, which they entered from the rear, was a large rectangle cluttered with folding chairs, a clothing rack and cabinets. On the far side he spotted Marnie sitting on a hard, wooden chair.

She looked pale beneath an oversize brownish-gray coat. Her knuckles were pale, too, as she clutched the edges of her seat.

"Are you sick?" Tom hurried to her.

"No." She regarded him tensely.

"I think I'll go see what Mike's up to." Betty headed for the exit.

Tom pulled a chair close to Marnie's and took her gloved hands in his. "Something's troubling you."

"Yes." She swallowed hard.

"And you carefully chose this dramatic moment to spring it on me."

His attempt at humor fell flat. Her only response was a nod.

What on earth was going on? "Having second thoughts?"

She shook her head.

"A bad case of laryngitis?"

"Oh, Tom, I wasn't trying to keep it secret. I couldn't seem to find the right way to tell you!"

He brought her hand to his lips. Not very personal, kissing a glove, but it seemed to reassure her a little. "Well, you can tell me now."

"I didn't plan this," she said miserably.

"Plan what?"

"We're pregnant."

His brain stumbled over the word *we*. Maybe he'd been speaking too many different languages this past week or maybe he was jet-lagged, but at first Tom couldn't quite grasp her meaning. "'We' who?"

"What do you mean, 'we who'?" Marnie stared as if he'd taken leave of his senses.

Finally, as if it had just arrived from a distant planet, the word *pregnant* hit home. His lungs went hollow, and Tom barely squeezed out, "You mean we're going to have a baby?"

She made a little noise in the affirmative.

He yearned to say something intelligent. Suave. Sophisticated. Instead he said, "Really? Are you sure?"

"Of course I am!"

He rushed on. "Have you seen a doctor? Is it okay for you to walk down the aisle? I could carry you."

"Tom!"

"What?"

"I'm having a baby, not a hernia. And I'm going to have it in about five months, not right now."

"I know that." He hadn't fully absorbed it, though. In fact, Tom felt so off center he was grateful to be sitting down.

"You aren't angry?"

Finally he understood. She was nervous because for so long he hadn't wanted children. "I told you, I changed my mind about kids."

"You didn't want them right away," she reminded him, her brown eyes glistening.

"Theoretically, no," Tom admitted. "I hoped for more time alone with you and Cody. But now that there's actually a baby on the way—can you feel it move yet?"

"No," she said. "A few more weeks, the doctor says."

"Well, it's...great." The word was inadequate to express the excitement spreading through Tom.

He knew, objectively, that the birth of a baby meant sleepless nights and hard work. But the wonder, the miracle of it, nearly overwhelmed him.

"You don't mind?" Marnie's voice quavered.

He longed to crush her against him, but he didn't dare risk hurting the baby. "Are you kidding? I'm thrilled! How about if we name it after your parents? Nicholas if it's a boy, and if it's a girl, well, Mary Anne sounds so much like Marnie, it might cause confusion. How about Anne Marie?"

''I can't believe you're choosing names already!'' Her eyes remained suspiciously wet, but this time, he hoped, with joy.

''How do fathers usually react when they get the news?''

''How should I know?''

He frowned as something else struck him. ''By the way, why are you wearing a raincoat?''

''Because you're not supposed to see me in my wedding—''

The outer door flew open and Jolene marched in. ''Everybody's ready! What's holding up the show?'' She gaped at Tom, which was probably the first time he'd ever seen Jolene taken aback. ''You're not supposed to be in here!''

''We're pregnant,'' he said.

''We are?'' She turned to her granddaughter, who nodded confirmation. ''Well, let's get you two married, for Pete's sake! Some of us haven't entirely forgotten about propriety.'' Her grin belied the sharp words.

''Sounds good to me.'' Tom helped Marnie to her feet. ''Don't make her walk too fast, okay? She's in a—what's the phrase?—a delicate condition.''

''I'll try not to run her three or four times around the cow pasture,'' snapped Jolene. ''Now get a move on, boy.''

Tom went to give Norbert and Mike the go-ahead. As he took his place by the altar, his mind buzzed over all that Marnie had said, and Granny, too.

When Marnie appeared, walking down the aisle between her grandmother and new grandfather, he agonized over every step. Afraid she might stumble or suffer a premature pain.

Head high, she arrived at the altar and handed her bouquet of tiny pink roses to her best friend. Then she laid her hand on Tom's arm and gazed up at him with pure happiness.

''Hi, Mommy!'' said Cody from where he stood beside Tom.

''Hi, sweetheart,'' she said with a smile so wide it nearly took wings, and Tom realized in a rush that his heart was freer than he'd dreamed possible.

Free to give itself to Marnie and to treasure her always. Free to love her and Cody and all the children they would ever have, for all the years to come.

If you enjoyed what you just read,
then we've got an offer you can't resist!

Take 2 bestselling
love stories FREE!
Plus get a FREE surprise gift!

Clip this page and mail it to Harlequin Reader Service®

IN U.S.A.
3010 Walden Ave.
P.O. Box 1867
Buffalo, N.Y. 14240-1867

IN CANADA
P.O. Box 609
Fort Erie, Ontario
L2A 5X3

YES! Please send me 2 free Harlequin American Romance® novels and my free surprise gift. Then send me 4 brand-new novels every month, which I will receive months before they're available in stores. In the U.S.A., bill me at the bargain price of $3.34 plus 25¢ delivery per book and applicable sales tax, if any*. In Canada, bill me at the bargain price of $3.71 plus 25¢ delivery per book and applicable taxes**. That's the complete price and a savings of over 10% off the cover prices—what a great deal! I understand that accepting the 2 free books and gift places me under no obligation ever to buy any books. I can always return a shipment and cancel at any time. Even if I never buy another book from Harlequin, the 2 free books and gift are mine to keep forever. So why not take us up on our invitation. You'll be glad you did!

154 HEN CNEX
354 HEN CNEY

Name	(PLEASE PRINT)	
Address	Apt.#	
City	State/Prov.	Zip/Postal Code

* Terms and prices subject to change without notice. Sales tax applicable in N.Y.
** Canadian residents will be charged applicable provincial taxes and GST.
  All orders subject to approval. Offer limited to one per household.
  ® are registered trademarks of Harlequin Enterprises Limited.

AMER99   ©1998 Harlequin Enterprises Limited

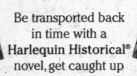

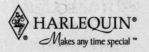

**Starting December 1999,
a brand-new series about
fatherhood from**

HARLEQUIN®

A M E R I C A N ◆ R O M A N C E®

THE
DADDY
CLUB

Three charming stories
about dads and kids...
and the women who
make their families
complete!

Available December 1999
FAMILY TO BE (#805)
by Linda Cajio

Available January 2000
A PREGNANCY AND A PROPOSAL (#809)
by Mindy Neff

Available February 2000
FOUR REASONS FOR FATHERHOOD (#813)
by Muriel Jensen

Available at your favorite retail outlet.

HARLEQUIN®
Makes any time special™

EXTRA! EXTRA!

The book all your favorite authors are raving about is finally here!

The 1999 Harlequin and Silhouette coupon book.

Each page is alive with savings that can't be beat!

Getting this incredible coupon book is as easy as 1, 2, 3.

1. During the months of November and December 1999 buy any 2 Harlequin or Silhouette books.

2. Send us your name, address and 2 proofs of purchase (cash receipt) to the address below.

3. Harlequin will send you a coupon book worth $10.00 off future purchases of Harlequin or Silhouette books in 2000.

Send us 3 cash register receipts as proofs of purchase and we will send you 2 coupon books worth a total saving of $20.00 (limit of 2 coupon books per customer).

Saving money has never been this easy.

Please allow 4-6 weeks for delivery. Offer expires December 31, 1999.

I accept your offer! Please send me (a) coupon booklet(s):

Name: _____

Address: _____ City: _____

State/Prov.: _____ Zip/Postal Code: _____

Send your name and address, along with your cash register receipts as proofs of purchase, to:

In the U.S.: Harlequin Books, P.O. Box 9057, Buffalo, N.Y. 14269

In Canada: Harlequin Books, P.O. Box 622, Fort Erie, Ontario L2A 5X3

Order your books and accept this coupon offer through our web site
http://www.romance.net
Valid in U.S. and Canada only.

PHQ4994R